Pirates, Ghosts, and Coastal Lore
The Best of Judge Whedbee

Pirates, Ghosts, and Coastal Lore

The Best of Judge Whedbee

Charles Harry Whedbee

Published by John F. Blair, Publisher

The paper in this book meets the guidelines
for permanence and durability of the
Committee on Production Guidelines for
Book Longevity of the Council on Library Resources.

Background jacket image—
Cape Hatteras Lighthouse, Buxton
Courtesy of NC Division of Tourism, Film and Sports Development

Image of skull taken from the cover of *Outer Banks Tales to Remember*,
photograph by Bernard Carpenter

Library of Congress Cataloging-in-Publication Data

Whedbee, Charles Harry.
Pirates, ghosts, and coastal lore : the best of Judge Whedbee / by Charles Harry Whedbee.
p. cm.
ISBN 0-89587-295-1 (alk. paper)
1. Tales—North Carolina—Outer Banks. 2. Legends—North Carolina—Outer Banks. 3. Ghost stories, American—North Carolina—Outer Banks. I. Title.
GR110.N8W485 2004
398.2'09756'102—dc22
2003020354

Design by Debra Long Hampton

Contents

Introduction

In June 1966, publisher John F. Blair asked his newest author, Charles Harry Whedbee, for some biographical information. In reply, Whedbee wrote Blair a four-page letter that concluded with a gem of modesty: "This reminds me of the man who asked another for the time of day and got a lecture on how to build a clock. I guess I have told you much more than you wanted about my inconsequential life."

We should all lead such inconsequential lives.

Whedbee was born in Greenville, North Carolina, in 1911. When he was two months old, his mother took him in her arms across the sound to Nags Head on the Outer Banks, where his uncle owned one of the original thirteen cottages that comprised the famous Unpainted Aristocracy. It was a trip Whedbee would make often until his death in 1990.

In the early days, families went to Nags Head as soon as school let out and stayed until it resumed in the fall. And they brought their household possessions with them, including the chickens and cows. There were no indoor bathrooms, no air conditioning, and no television back then. All the same, Whedbee recognized that he was "living in the eastern suburb of heaven on earth." He and the other children roamed the deserted beach as far as their legs would take them. At night, the vacationers took turns telling tales. Anyone who couldn't come up with a story was dipped in the Atlantic. "I always had enough stories," Whedbee said.

Whedbee completed college and law school at the University of North Carolina at Chapel Hill, aided by a football scholarship and several part-time jobs.

He was just embarking on his legal career when he was involved in a head-on automobile collision in the early 1930s. Whedbee suffered a fractured skull and legs broken in several places. Pronounced dead at the hospital, he was brought to the undertaker, who filled out a death certificate and was merely awaiting a doctor's signature when he heard a moan. "It was me," Whedbee said. "They rushed me back to the hospital. You hear people say they hear all this celestial music. I didn't hear anything." He was unconscious for a month and confined to a wheelchair for a year.

In the mid-1930s, Whedbee was elected solicitor of the County Court of Pitt County. Following that came a stint as judge of the Municipal Recorders Court of Greenville. Ultimately, he served as chief district court judge of the Third Judicial District, an office from which he retired in 1980.

He always treated the defendants who appeared before him with the respect due people who had simply made a mistake. "Judge Whedbee had the best judicial temperament of anyone I ever saw on the bench," remarked a fellow jurist.

Whedbee was also noted for his pioneering efforts in work-release and community-service sentencing, doling out punishments innovatively tailored to the crimes. Confronted with college students stopped for driving over a hundred miles an hour, Whedbee sentenced the young men to lose their licenses for a year and to spend ten consecutive Saturday nights in the local emergency room, seeing the wreck victims and the despair of family members. "Thus, we did not interfere with their education, but we did succeed in bringing home to them the possible consequences of their conduct," he explained. When two male students stole a pair of dresses from a secondhand store, Whedbee made them pay double for the items, put them on—complete with feminine undergarments—and walk up and down the city's main street at noon on Saturday.

It was 1938 when Whedbee first dipped his toe in the media waters, moonlighting as a news commentator on a local radio station.

In 1963, he was asked to substitute on a morning show called *Carolina Today* on Greenville's television station while one of the program's regulars was in the hospital. Whedbee took the opportunity to tell some of the Outer Banks stories he'd heard during his many summers at Nags Head. The station received such a volume of mail in praise of his tale-telling that he was invited to remain even after the man he was substituting for returned to the air. "He had a way of telling a story that really captured me," said one of the program's co-hosts. "Whether he was talking about a sunset, a ghost, or a shipwreck, I was there, living every minute of it."

Word traveled as far as Winston-Salem, where John F. Blair proposed to Whedbee that he compile his stories in book form. Whedbee welcomed the challenge, though his expectations for the manuscript that became *Legends of the Outer Banks and Tar Heel Tidewater* were modest. "I wrote it out of a love for this region and the people whom I'd known all my life," he said. "I didn't think it would sell a hundred copies."

From the very first sentence of the foreword, Whedbee stamped the collection with his inimitable style: "You are handed herewith a small pod or school of legends about various portions of that magical region known as the Outer Banks of North Carolina as well as stories from other sections of the broad bays, sounds, and estuaries that make up tidewater Tarheelia."

The Lost Colony, Indians, Blackbeard, an albino porpoise that guided ships into harbor—the tales in that volume form the core of Outer Banks folklore. Whedbee liked to tell people that his stories were of three kinds: those he knew to be true, those he believed to be true, and those he fabricated. But despite much prodding, he never revealed which were which. "Some of the biggest laughs I get is for some old-timer to say, 'Well, Charlie, I read such and such a story, and I know *that* one is not true.' And chances are, that'll turn out to be the very one which *is* true. And believe you me, on the Outer Banks, anything can happen."

Legends of the Outer Banks went through three printings in 1966, its first year. Demand for Whedbee's tales and the author's supply of good material were such that further volumes were inevitable. *The Flaming Ship of Ocracoke & Other Tales of the Outer Banks* was published in 1971, *Outer Banks Mysteries & Seaside Stories* in 1978, *Outer Banks Tales to Remember* in 1985, and *Blackbeard's Cup and Stories of the Outer Banks* in 1989. Altogether, the five books have gone through fifty-eight printings and sold more than 205,000 copies. Now in its nineteenth printing, *Legends of the Outer Banks* has sold 111,000 copies.

Indeed, Whedbee's stories proved so popular that they generated their own legends.

Take "Blackbeard's Cup." In it, Whedbee recounts the day more than half a century earlier when he and a fellow law student attended a secret meeting at Blackbeard's castle on Ocracoke Island, during which they drank from a strange, oversized, silver-plated cup they were told was the skull of Blackbeard himself. When Whedbee offered a thousand-dollar reward for anyone who could give him access to the cup long enough to determine its authenticity, letters came in from far and wide, and the media lapped it up.

Or "The Flaming Ship of Ocracoke." John F. Blair was so taken with the story that he closed the office and brought his entire staff 250 miles across North Carolina, then two and a half hours aboard a ferry to the lonely beach where the doomed vessel was due to sail brightly past on the night of the new moon in September.

Even Whedbee's final act was the stuff of legend. After the death of the judge and his wife, the royalties from his books were conveyed by will to his Nags Head church, St. Andrew's By-The-Sea, a legacy that continues to this day.

But more important were the personal connections he forged while telling his stories and promoting his books. Few people who met Judge Whedbee at an autographing forgot his enthusiasm for the places of which he wrote. Those readers who discovered him in the late 1960s and early 1970s introduced him to their children as soon as they were old enough. And those children have since brought forth a third generation of Whedbee lovers. The popularity of the judge's tales is undiminished today.

And so it is fitting that in this, the fiftieth year of John F. Blair, Publisher, the company should release this volume of the best stories of Charles Harry Whedbee, coastal ambassador and foremost raconteur of the Outer Banks.

Pirates, Ghosts, and Coastal Lore
The Best of Judge Whedbee

The Ghost Deer of Roanoke

from *Legends of the Outer Banks and Tar Heel Tidewater*

Since time immemorial and up to the beginning of the twentieth century, the Outer Banks of the Old North State were remarkable for a profusion of grapevines. There is something about the air and about the minerals in the soil that seems to grow beautiful grapes on luxuriant vines. There was a time within the memory of men still living when the grapes grew down so close to the sea that the very ocean swells would break upon them in time of storm. It was great sport for the more daring of the young boys in that section to grasp a stout grapevine and swing, Tarzan-like, out over the ocean shallows. Roanoke Island, itself, was partially covered with these vines.

One of the very oldest of these grapevines grew on the eastern shore line of that island. It had a main stem as big as a man's body, and the place where it grew was known over many parts of the world as the Mother Vineyard. Slips of cuttings from this Mother Vineyard were carried to England and to France and there planted and tended. Many of the slips are said to have been carried to California, where they grew, and still grow, in great profusion.

Up until a few years prior to this writing, this Mother Vineyard was kept on a reduced scale, and some very excellent wine was made from its grapes. The name is still carried on some of the highway signs on Roanoke Island, but most of the vineyard has now given way to a very beautiful housing project on the shore line of this storied island. The subdivision is now known by the name of the Mother Vineyard. *Sic transit gloria.*

Captain Martin Johnson, who used to run the steamer *Trenton* from Elizabeth City to Nags Head and Manteo in the early nineteen-twenties, knew the ancient legend of that vine. It was a reverie-inducing fable he would tell to the children of the passengers of his fine craft to while away some of the long hours as the *Trenton* churned her way through the cola-colored waters of Albemarle Sound. I heard the same legend related many years ago as a group of smallish boys sat around a campfire on the banks of a broad river where the Matchapungo Indians once had a town. Talk about goose bumps and furtive looks into the dark forest beyond the fire's circle of light!

The story begins in the time when the John White settlers first came to Roanoke in the year 1587. As you know, Virginia Dare was born, both she and Chief Manteo were baptized into the Christian faith, and Governor White set sale for England to bring back supplies but was unable to return for three full years.

According to the legend, in the autumn of the second year of the City of Raleigh, hostile Indians under Chief Wanchese attacked the city and the fort. There had been many disputes by Wanchese and his followers with the leaders of the colonists. The fact that Governor White did not return as he had promised caused Wanchese to believe that the colony had been deserted, and he grew more insolent as the months went by. Finally the chief swore a great oath to kill every colonist, down to the last woman and child, and thus rid his island of the hated foreigners. Retribution was not to be feared from the men in the "great canoes with wings" since they had obviously forgotten this little band. So it was that Wanchese sat down and planned the complete destruction of the white settlement and the murder of all its inhabitants.

The raiders attacked at dawn and without warning. Several of the colonists were killed before they could reach the safety of the fort, but those within that rude battlement managed to close the doors and set up an answering fire with their muskets. Thus the siege of Fort Raleigh began. Poisoned arrows were used by Wanchese's warriors, and every time a settler showed himself atop the fort, he was the immediate target for these deadly missiles. With the approach of night, fire arrows were brought into play. In the twilight many buildings within the enclosure became flaming torches illuminating the desperate scene. Not knowing how long they could hold out and wanting to conserve their water for drinking purposes, the colonists attempted to take down the buildings that were afire and thus prevent the flames from spreading while they replied with musket shot to the onslaughts of the Indians.

Chief Manteo had been on a fishing expedition that day, and Wanchese believed he would remain away for several days at the very least. The friendly Indian had taken a small party of his tribe and had gone southward in the direction of Hatteras. He had found fishing no good at all and was returning in the dusk when he saw the red glow in the sky.

Sensing trouble from so large a blaze, he redoubled his speed; and as he drew near the fort, he began to hear the sounds of musket fire as well as the shrill, wild cry of the war-crazed attackers. Trouble had been brewing for some time with the dissident braves under the other chief's command, and Manteo at once grasped what was happening. He realized that his small fishing party was badly outnumbered by the Indians whom he could see leaping and screaming in the light of the burning buildings. Knowing full well that the colonists could not last until he went for reinforcements, he determined to try to help them escape.

Gaining entrance to the fort by a secret tunnel which opened on the banks of the Sound, Manteo and his small band urged the colonists to flee under cover of darkness while yet they could. This they did. There was no time to bury their dead and no time to take more than the most meager personal belongings. Hurriedly the survivors crept single file through the tunnel and down to the shore where the canoes of the fishing party were waiting.

As Ananias and Eleanor Dare with their infant daughter, Virginia, followed Manteo through the dense woods which screened the tunnel's mouth, Ananias bethought him of the agreement with Governor White that the colonists would carve the name of their destination on a tree if they had to flee Fort Raleigh. Thereby, rescue parties could the more easily find them.

Over Manteo's strong protest, Ananias insisted on stopping before a great oak tree. He whipped out his sheath knife, quickly stripped the bark off a portion of the oak about head-high, and began to carve upon the bared surface. Three letters only did he carve, *C R O,* when a lone straggler from Wanchese's attacking force saw him and, with a triumphant scream, shot a poisoned arrow through this heart, killing him on the spot. The return fire from Manteo's bow came only a split second later. It, too, was fatal, killing the attacker in his tracks and gaining a few more seconds of precious time before the besiegers would find that their quarry was escaping.

Fearful that this new commotion might bring others of the attacking force, Manteo now insisted on immediate flight. At first Eleanor Dare was reluctant to leave the body of her fallen husband. It was not until Manteo reminded her of her duty to the infant, Virginia, that she tearfully agreed to go. To reassure her, the noble chief made the sign of the cross upon his own forehead and with his finger made the same sign on the forehead of the infant. Then, lifting his eyes to the sky, he pledged lifelong protection to the distraught mother and her baby.

Swiftly now they made their way to the waiting canoes, as swiftly boarded them, and pushed off into the night. The strong arms of Manteo and of his companions at the paddles sped them on into the trackless expanse of water north of the Island. All night they traveled lest Wanchese's braves might pursue them in war canoes. As dawn was beginning to color the east, they came to the home of Manteo's people. Later that same day they were joined by the other survivors of the attack; and, falling down in the homes of their rescuers, they slept the sleep of exhaustion. For the time being, their lives were safe. No force of Wanchese was strong enough to attack this village.

The next day a great council was held. Manteo called together the subchiefs of his people and pleaded with them to receive the white people into the tribe as their own. The Indian women, meanwhile, were much taken with little Virginia Dare. They could not understand her fair, white skin, and they seemed fascinated by it. She was not dark-skinned like the Indians. Moreover, her hair was a soft golden color, such as they had never seen on mortal being. "Little snow-papoose" they called her and wondered among themselves whether she would melt away with the return of the summer sun as the snow did.

The council heeded Manteo's plea and agreed to accept the

white colonists into the tribe as blood brothers. Small cuts were made in the arms of each of the whites and of a corresponding number of Indians. Then the arm of each colonist was bound to the arm of his Indian counterpart and the blood permitted to mingle so that they did, indeed, become blood brothers. After only a few minutes the bonds were cut and the arms freed. Thus did necessity make Indians of them all.

With the practicality of people who live close to nature, the first thing the red men did was to help these newcomers build homes of their own. Then they taught the whites to hunt the red deer and to fish for the great fish that swam in the sounds and bays. All this and much more the people of Manteo's tribe taught the colonists. The new arrivals, for their part, taught the Indians about the white man's God and about Christ and His compassion for all people. In time they also taught them how to build a two-story house, a thing never before heard of by the Indians. The colonists also instructed their hosts in the use of a musket and showed them how to read or "speak from a book," as well as how to use crossbows, breastplates, and helmets. All in all, it was an exchange of vast benefit to both sides, and the adopted members fitted well into the life of the tribe.

The child, Virginia Dare, was the marvel and the cynosure of all the Indians. As she grew into young womanhood, her character and her personality developed to equal her beauty, and she became the favorite of all who knew her. With her fair complexion, deep blue eyes, and hair the color of wild honey, she soon became a sort of white priestess to them. "Winona-Ska" they called her, and they listened intently as she told them of her mother's homeland and its ways and of her belief in God and His mercy to all His children. Her most difficult task was to teach them not to worship her, for this they were most ready to do. They brought all their troubles to her and sought her aid in settling disputes. Her counsel was accepted by them on all manner of things. On many occasions she settled the most bitter arguments simply by appearing on the scene and, with an admonitory hand, making the sign of the cross over them.

All the braves of Manteo's tribe loved Winona-Ska. They brought her presents of red deer and foxes and delicious fish which they speared in the sounds. One of them, however, outdid all the others in his devotion and in his tireless efforts to please her. This was Okisko, a brave of noble blood who was only a year or two her senior but already one of the mightiest hunters of the tribe.

Being an Indian brave, he was troubled greatly by his belief that it would be unmanly to speak of his love, and yet he wanted most desperately to show this goddess-woman how he felt. Each day he tried in some new way to show his love yet never spoke of it. On one occasion he even tried to affix to his canoe the wings of a huge goose he had killed, hoping that he would thus be able to sail the small craft as she had told him her people sailed. With such magnificent wings on his canoe, he thought, he might sail a mighty journey eastward and find her people for her. Even though his fellow braves mocked him for this and for other similar acts, Okisko persisted in them, the only way he knew to show his love.

Winona-Ska, with a woman's insight, saw immediately what was going on, and she realized what the situation was. She was deeply touched. She liked Oksiko very much but felt no love for him other than she might have felt for a brother, had she been lucky enough to have one. And with an insight beyond his sex and beyond his years, Okisko contented himself with waiting. His hope and his belief was that someday love would awaken within the heart of Winona-Ska and that she would then turn to him as her choice for a mate.

The fair beauty of Winona-Ska was not lost on others of the tribe either. Old Chico, the magician and shaman, looked long and searchingly at her. As he gazed, his youth seemed to return; the fires of long-forgotten young manhood seemed to rekindle in his breast. Yes, he, too, loved this young maiden. He loved her in his own way, he wanted her as his wife, and he set about to woo her. He would cover himself with bright war paint and place huge feathers on his head and arms. Thus decorated, he would strut and posture before her like some great, outlandish bird. He would make great magic by rattling dried melon seeds in a gourd and would dance fierce dances for what he hoped would be her pleasure.

Kindheartedly, Winona-Ska smiled upon his efforts but mostly to keep the others from laughing. Although old enough to be her father, Chico grew wildly jealous of her. When he would see her smile at the young Okisko, his very soul would burn with jealousy and rage. Sick with desire and hopelessness, he finally determined that, if he could not have her as his wife, then no man would.

Although he had not had occasion to use his knowledge of magic in recent years, Chico had been a great magician in his day. He knew all the ancient spells handed down from his great-grandfather, who had also been the great-grandfather of the evil Wanchese. Chico knew the language of the lost spirits and could communicate with them. It was even rumored he could talk with the Evil One Himself. The old medicine man also knew many sinister potions and supernatural recipes whereby man might control a part of nature itself, and it was this course that he finally decided to pursue. By the use of his own black magic, he would once and for all insure that Winona-Ska would be his, or else she would be no man's.

With a great deal of effort Chico set about collecting from

the waters as many pearls from the abundant mussels as he could find. Not ordinary pearls, mind you. For his dark purpose he required pied or speckled pearls which seemed to glow like fireflies with their own eerie light and to emit a sort of purple incandescence. Such pearls are known by magicians to be the souls of water nymphs who have disobeyed the King of the Sea and, for punishment, have been sentenced to imprisonment in the shells of mussels. These water nymphs are very grateful when freed by mortal men, and they will do anything the liberator asks of them, whether the request be for good or evil. When he had a sufficient number of these liberated nymphs under his control, Chico revealed his plan to them. He told them what he plotted to do to the golden Winona-Ska and demanded their help in his scheme as the price of their freedom. True to their natures and obligated to him for freeing them, they promised to help him.

This being accomplished, Chico hid his pied pearls and set about to build a large canoe. He fashioned it with great care, so that it floated with grace upon the waters like a large swan. It was a beautiful vessel. When it was finished, he asked Winona-Ska to take a trip with him to Roanoke so the canoe could be blessed by the spirits there. He assured her that the trip could be made within a few hours and that, if they left at dawn, they would return long before the evening cooking fires were lit. Although she had been back to these scenes of her early childhood many times, Winona-Ska agreed to go with Chico to keep from hurting his feelings. After all, the weather was beautiful, the water was calm, and the canoe was a new and fine one. She was flattered to be asked to take the first trip in such a handsome craft.

Now, indeed, was Chico's plot working to perfection. Although the sea nymphs have no power on water—for there the

Sea King is the absolute ruler—once on land, their powers are tremendous, and their magic is so fierce that only a greater magic can withstand it. Thus Chico had schemed to get his beautiful prey to go with him across the water and then to land a good distance from their village, so that no one might be near to witness the evil deed he had in mind.

Chico had sung and chanted to each of his speckled pearls and had bathed them in a magic potion. He had then strung them into a lovely necklace, giving each pearl an explicit reminder of what he expected of her. As he and Winona-Ska glided over the water toward the island of Roanoke, he gave the necklace to her; and she, greatly pleasured by the beauty of his gift, placed the magic necklace around her neck. Unsuspecting, she fingered the pearls and looked at them in admiration, for they seemed to glow with their own light. She would, of course, give the lovely ornament back to Chico. It was too fine a gift to accept from one to whom she was not betrothed. For the time, though, she would wear it and enjoy its unreal beauty before giving it back on their return to the home village.

As they approached the sandy shores of Roanoke, Chico drove his paddle deep in the waters of the Sound and sent his new boat fairly flying over the calm surface, so that it ran half its length out upon the sandy shore before stopping. Lightfooted and happy, Winona-Ska sprang from the canoe and onto the sandy beach; and there, after leaving just one human footprint, she changed into a magnificent snow-white doe and sprang away into the forest.

Along the shores of that wooded island, the evil laughter of old Chico rang out and echoed back and forth among the pine and yaupon trees. Success was his! Winona-Ska had indeed now been placed far beyond the powers of any ordinary man to possess her. Thus was Chico's evil oath fulfilled.

Meanwhile, in the village the Indians waited long for Winona-Ska to return. No one had seen her leave with Chico, and Chico kept his own counsel. At his request, she had told no one of her plans lest such a disclosure spoil the blessing of the canoe. Far and wide the men searched for their lost high priestess. Many and long were the journeys they made, but all in vain. Winona-Ska had vanished as though the very earth had swallowed her up. Finally the search was given up, and she was mourned as forever lost.

Shortly thereafter there began a legend of a strange white doe that roamed the woods of Roanoke. The other deer looked upon her as a sort of leader, the story went, and followed wherever she led. Furthermore, no arrow was able to kill, or even to hit, this white doe. Many braves coveted the white fur for a ceremonial robe, and some of the best hunters of several tribes had tried to kill her but in vain. She seemed to lead a truly charmed life.

When this became known, the older women of the tribe began to put two and two together. Firm believers in witchcraft, they saw the similarity between the vanished white maiden and the sudden appearance of the white doe. Since they remembered that Old Chico had been a great magician, they gossiped that it must have been Chico and his black magic that had caused the disappearance of the girl; that Chico must have bewitched Winona-Ska and changed her into a white doe. It takes only one repetition of gossip to change "it must have been" to "it was"; so was it then as it is now. By the third retelling it was being stated as a fact that Chico was responsible.

Okisko heard this gossip, and his heart was glad. He also readily accepted this explanation of the disappearance of his beloved. Since Winona-Ska had been bewitched, perhaps he could find even greater magic to break the spell. First, though, the white doe should be captured for her own protection and then the magical antidote searched for. In the days that followed, the young brave traveled often to Roanoke to try to capture the white doe but without any semblance of success. He could not even come close to capturing her. No matter how cunning his traps, she would always avoid them. It seemed as though she could read his mind. On several occasions when he caught sight of the splendid animal, she seemed to look directly at him with a great sorrow in her soft eyes before she turned and faded away into the forest.

Almost physically sick with frustration and believing now that he could never capture the white doe without the aid of a great magic, Okisko packed his canoe and traveled all the way to Weapomeoc, the Meeting of the Waters. Here was a great Indian settlement of Okisko's nation, which was the home of a mighty magician known as Wenaudon. Unknown to Okisko, there had long been bad feeling and much jealousy between the mighty Wenaudon and the wily Chico. Wenaudon was only too glad to be the instrument whereby his enemy might be embarrassed and made to look foolish. When he had heard Okisko's story, he immediately agreed to help him.

Taking Okisko aside into the forest where they could talk in secret, Wenaudon told him of a magic spring of water on Roanoke Island. It was a bubbling, natural fountain of fresh water where the sea nymphs held their revels and where they met their lovers. So enamoured were the nymphs of this spot that they had laid a spell upon the waters that would always make true lovers happy and secure. To drink of this magic spring was to have one's youth restored. He who bathed in the waters in the light of the full moon was given the power to undo all black magic and cancel out all evil spells. Having bathed in this spring when he was only an apprentice magician, Wenaudon knew of it, and he now prepared to share this knowledge with Okisko.

"First," he told the young visitor, "you must secure a tooth from the fierce hammerhead shark. It must be a long and narrow tooth, and very sharp. Then, within the triangle formed by the corners of the tooth, you must affix three purple mussel-pearls, one to each corner and each made bright with much rubbing and polishing. To this shark's tooth, you must affix an arrow shaft of witch-hazel wood that has never before been used as an arrow. To fletch this magic weapon, you must pluck just one feather from the wing of a living heron, then release the heron without further harm, and hide the arrow from all human sight. Let no one gaze upon it, and tell no one of your purpose. Then, when the moon is full, take the arrow from its hiding place and submerge it in the magic waters of the enchanted spring on Roanoke. There let it remain for three full nights while you stand guard. When the sun is rising on the third morning after its submerging, take the arrow in your hands thus and point it toward the rising sun. Pray to the Great Spirit that your arrow may free the gentle Winona-Ska from the evil charm and restore her to you.

"With this arrow you must then hunt the white doe. When you have brought her to bay, take care to shoot the arrow straight into her heart. Do not fear. She will not be harmed by your arrow. If your aim is true, the evil spell of Chico will be ended, and she will resume her human form."

Thus spoke Wenaudon to Okisko, who heeded every word and wrote it upon his heart. The young lover then made haste to return to his native village and thence go to Roanoke, where he began the preparation of his magic arrow. Each step was followed with care, and the arrow was finally completed, exactly as he had been instructed.

It also happened that, at this same time, the neighboring

chief, Wanchese, son of the old Chief Wanchese, called for a truce among all the tribes and announced a mighty hunt to celebrate the ending of hostilities. He proposed a smoking of the peace pipe among the nations and then a joint hunt, in which the quarry would be the fabled white doe of Roanoke. The brave who killed the white doe would be named the greatest hunter among them all.

Tired of senseless fighting, the other chiefs agreed although they only half trusted the word of this younger Wanchese. They remembered too well the treachery of the old Chief Wanchese, his father; and they feared the son might be too much like the father. Since no harm could come from an attempt at peace, however, it was decided to go along with the young Wanchese's plan, keeping a sharp eye out all the while for any sign of betrayal.

Now, this young Wanchese had as a gift from this father a silver arrowhead which Queen Elizabeth herself had given him upon his visit to England. The young chief fully believed that this lustrous arrowhead held some magic power. He planned to use it to kill the white doe himself and thus bring to his house the fame and the glory that such a feat would ensure.

The hunt was duly organized, and only braves of noble blood were allowed to participate. On the appointed day the princely hunters took to the woods—Okisko with his magic arrow and Wanchese with his silver-pointed dart. Though neither knew the other was near, both these mighty hunters spied the white doe at the same instant. She was standing perfectly still and gazing at the ruins of the ancient Fort Raleigh. Aiming carefully and with bated breath, Okisko and Wanchese each drew his powerful bow and, at the same instant, shot his special arrow at the beautiful target at a range so close it seemed impossible that either could miss. One arrow carried with it hope, love, and compassion. The other bore malice, greed, and cunning. The hunters were equally skilled and equally powerful, and both arrows pierced the heart of the white doe, making the shape of a cross as they did so. As the fates would have it, Okisko's arrow arrived at the target just a split second before the dart of Wanchese.

To the amazement of Wanchese, a silver mist seemed to envelop the white doe as, before his very eyes, she changed from a doe to a beautiful young woman with long, golden hair and bright blue eyes.

To the anguish of Okisko, as soon as his beloved resumed her human form, there was the silver-headed arrow piercing her heart. From its wound the bright red blood flowed down the side of Winona-Ska. Restored to her human form one instant, but mortally wounded the next, she slowly collapsed and fell prostrate on the forest floor.

Wanchese fled in terror at this sight, but Okisko ran to his beloved. He found that his magic arrow had, indeed, pierced the heart of Winona-Ska but had done no harm and, as Wenaudon had predicted, had accomplished her transformation. Wanchese's arrow, arriving a heartbeat later, had pierced the human heart and had broken the shark's-tooth point of the magic arrow.

In one wild and desperate attempt to save his Winona-Ska, Okisko seized his broken arrow and ran headlong back along the forest trail until he reached the enchanted spring. Here, in broad daylight, he plunged his magic arrow into the bubbling fountain and besought the Great Spirit that his beloved be spared. As Okisko knelt and looked at the splashing waters, the spring began to subside and to disappear into the ground. Before his anguished eyes, it dried up and vanished completely. Simultaneously, the arrow became fully rooted in the ground where the nymphs' enchanted spring had been. From the top and sides of the arrow, little green leaves began to appear. As they grew and unfolded before his eyes, they became the leaves of a grape-vine, and the witch-hazel staff turned into the main stem of the vine. When he returned to look for his Winona-Ska near the ruins of the fort, she was nowhere to be seen; but yonder, in the gathering dusk, he thought he saw the flash of a white deer bounding away. At least a part of his prayer had been answered. The white doe was restored to life, but never again could she be transformed into her human form. To this day, she is said to roam the woods of Roanoke and of the mainland as well, as impervious to modern guns as she was to bows and arrows. To try in any way to harm her is said to bring on the worst of fortune imaginable.

Over the years the grapevine grew and flourished, and the main stem became in time as thick as a man's body. Thus was the Mother Vineyard started, and thus was established the parent vine that has furnished slips and cuttings to be transplanted all over this country of ours, and in England and France as well.

It was claimed for years that, on a dark and moonless night, you could, if you listened very carefully, hear the lovely Winona-Ska crying for her lost love. There were even those who said that the blueness of some of the grapes was the very blueness in the eyes of that lovely maid who was born here many centuries before.

The Pirate Lights of Pamilico Sound

from *Legends of the Outer Banks and Tar Heel Tidewater*

Ocracoke and Portsmouth Islands are permeated with the ghost of Blackbeard, most famous of all American pirates. There is scarcely a beach on either Sound or ocean shore of these islands that has not echoed to the booming roar of his voice and felt the heavy tread of his tremendous boots. Ocracoke was his village, and he loved it with a fierce and jealous affection, which he obviously did not feel for Hatteras, although he frequently visited that island as well. It was on Ocracoke that this famous brigand lived, drank his rum, and roared his threats against British authority. Bath Town was another home he loved, but it was not near the sea, his natural habitat.

Blackbeard had good cause, he thought, to defy British authority. He was often heard to complain in a most profane manner about a king who would train an honest seaman in a way of life and then turn about and make it a crime to live that way of life. Born in Bristol, England, and christened Edward Drummond, he went to sea at an early age as a cabin boy. As a young man he served as a seaman aboard a British privateer in what is known to history as Queen Anne's War. Under this arrangement it was perfectly legal for, and the patriotic duty of, the captain of a ship licensed as a privateer to attack a merchant ship flying the flag of France, impress or imprison the merchantman's crew, and then share in the division of the captured ship's cargo. Of course, sometimes a Spanish flag was mistaken for a French one, but the wartime government of Britain was not inclined to quibble over technicalities. Under this arrangement the crown was spared the expense of paying the crew and of outfitting and supplying the ship, enemy shipping was destroyed or captured, and a portion of valuable cargoes was delivered to the official treasury. All that was necessary was a license as a privateer, and a captain became his own naval commander, his own tactician, and his own bookkeeper for the division of spoils. Some of the very best and bravest of English captains served at one time or another as privateers. The profits were huge.

When the war had come to an end, though, and peace was made with France, what had been patriotism became piracy; and this was the burden of Blackbeard's complaint—or at least so he said! At the war's end Edward Teach (he had changed his name from Drummond to Teach or Thatch or Tatch) was a lieutenant under a Captain Hornigold, a very successful privateer. The crown offered amnesty to all former privateersmen and/or pirates who would reform and swear an oath of law-abiding fealty to the king and, of course, surrender to the crown such captured ships as they were using.

Captain Hornigold decided to take the king's pardon. He moved ashore, took the oath, and settled down to enjoy the profits of his former occupation. Since Teach, however, had no accumulated wealth, he just kept possession of the ship that Hornigold had given him to command and set sail for the Americas to seek his own fortune. If there had been any doubt before, that act branded Edward Teach a pirate.

Renaming his vessel the *Queen Anne's Revenge* and recruiting as desperate and able a crew from the "brotherhood of the sea" as can well be imagined, he soon made a name for himself as the scourge of the Atlantic seaboard. He even took on the British man-of-war H.M.S. *Scarborough* and fought her on even terms for several hours before the *Scarborough* broke off the engagement and ran for cover. It was after this victory that Teach adopted the name "Blackbeard."

He was the possessor of a magnificent, bushy beard the color of jet. This hirsute adornment extended from just beneath his eyes all the way down to his waist, hiding his belt buckle. It was almost as wide as his barrel-shaped chest and served as a sort of banner or rallying flag for his henchmen in the thick of hand-to-hand battle. Since Teach was nearly seven feet in height, this expanse of beard was awe-inspiring to friend and foe alike. To make his appearance even more frightful, he would twist little pigtails in his beard and tie them with red ribbons. Then he would coil a snakelike, slow-burning match of punk around his head just over his ears and under the brim of his hat. When both ends of this decoration were lit and smoking and his white teeth were gleaming in an evil grin amidst that heavy black beard, our pirate might well have been mistaken for the devil himself.

Completely fearless, this giant of a pirate roamed the Atlantic at will, taking as he went prizes in the form of noble ships, which he either sunk or else manned with a prize crew of pirates. Never one to hang back from the thick of personal combat, Blackbeard always led the charge of the fearsome boarding parties that swarmed from the deck of the *Revenge* onto the scuppers of the victim. The sight of this monster with what looked like blazing horns protruding from his brow, red ribbons bedecking a huge beard, a pistol in one hand and a gleaming sword in the other, was enough to frighten any defender half to death to begin with. Even the mention of his name was enough to strike fear into the hearts of merchants and seamen alike. At one time he actually blockaded the City of Charleston, South Carolina, with his one ship and forced that proud city to pay a ransom of a fortune in drugs and medicines before he sailed away, keeping his word not to put the city to the torch once the ransom was paid.

Blackbeard's favorite territory, though, seemed to be Ocracoke and Portsmouth. He could sell his captured cargoes to the merchants there much cheaper than they could buy elsewhere and without their having to pay a farthing to British tariff. This was the territory that he considered to be his home base. Here he went to careen his ships, repair battle damage, and fit them out for more piracy. On Ocracoke Island he built himself a large and comfortable house. Two stories high and containing many large rooms, this house became known through the years as "Blackbeard's Castle." This is where the pirate lived when he came ashore and where he counted and arranged his treasure before moving it to hiding places which, according to his own statement shortly before his death, were known only to the devil and to the pirate captain himself. Blackbeard's large castle was abandoned after his death to grow up in weeds and was almost completely hidden by the undergrowth. It was finally torn down in the name of "progress" to make way for a more modern structure.

It was near Ocracoke Inlet that an incident took place which resulted in the permanent crippling of Israel Hands, first mate of the pirate band. It seems that Teach and Hands were sitting at a table with a third brigand drinking rum. They were below decks in their ship, and a single candle on the table gave a faint light to the scene. In a "test of courage" Blackbeard pulled his loaded pistol from his belt and held it under the table. Vowing to shoot any man who did not run, he then blew out the candle and started counting. The crewman broke and ran, but Israel Hands remained sitting and continued to drink from his goblet. With no compunction whatsoever, Blackbeard pulled the trigger and blasted away in the direction of the chair in which he had last seen his trusted mate before blowing out the candle. The slug hit the unlucky Israel in the knee and ranged upward into his thigh. Rum was administered, and the bullet was cut out of his leg then and there, but Israel Hands remained crippled from that wound as long as he lived. The rugged pirate was the prototype from which Robert Louis Stevenson created his fictional pirate of the story *Treasure Island.* Stevenson even gave his creation the name of this first mate of the Blackbeard ship. Present-day charts of the water around Ocracoke still show "Teach's Hole," where the drunken master pirate's aim in the darkness was still accurate enough to cripple his good friend.

At one time in his career Blackbeard apparently decided to give up piracy. He had amassed a goodly amount of treasure to live on, and he got the idea that he would like to live ashore. Sailing into Bath Town, he notified the British authorities that he was reformed, that he wished to mend his evil ways and take the oath of loyalty to the crown. Full pardon was granted to "our newly loyal subject" by the authorities, and he gave up his ship and bought a house on the point of Bath Creek. He even married the sixteen-year-old daughter of a local farmer and made her mistress of his home. What, if anything, he did about wives he was reputed to have in Elizabeth City, in Edenton, and in Ocracoke is unknown, but it is unlikely the four ladies ever met one another.

A "gentlemen's life ashore" apparently meant one long drunken spree for our hero, for that is exactly how he lived it. Shamefully mistreating his young wife and opening his house and his purse to any and all comers, he dissipated in a short time the tidy fortune he had brought ashore. Then, too, he began to have a genuine hunger for the sea and for shipboard life. He was a child of the sea, and he never felt really at home unless he was walking the deck of an ocean-going vessel. At length he bought and fitted out such a boat and told all and sundry she was to be used as an honest seagoing merchantman. Naming his new craft the *Adventure,* he never did explain the meaning of the gun-ports along both her sides, shutters that swung open to reveal the ugly snouts of cannon mounted 'tween decks.

Off to sea sailed the *Adventure* with Edward Teach as her skipper, and back she came, time after time, towing crewless ships that Teach claimed to have found abandoned on the open sea with cargoes untouched. He still insisted that he was an honest merchant seaman who had had the extreme good luck to find his prizes floating derelict on the ocean. Once again his fortunes began to rise.

After a few months of this pretense, Blackbeard tired of the sham and openly returned to pirating. That way he didn't have to kill all the captured crews, and many of them came to be valued crewmen on his raider. With complete impartiality, our pirate preyed on the shipping of all nations. He would as soon sink a British ship as a Spanish one, nor was the commerce of the American merchants safe from his depredations.

Then Edward Teach's overleaping ambition proved his undoing. Not content with the fruit of his own labors, he conceived the grandiose scheme of fortifying Ocracoke Island and making it into a haven and refuge for all pirate ships. He himself was to reign there as a sort of king of the pirates while they were in his stronghold. As a fee for such sanctuary, he planned to charge each incoming ship a percentage of the prize money for the privilege of membership in the club.

This plan would probably have succeeded, because Teach was a master strategist and would have had capable help. The ship owners and merchants of the Carolinas heard of this dream, however, and were appalled at the prospect. Despairing of any help whatsoever from Governor Eden in Bath, they sent a delegation to Governor Spotswood of the colony of Virginia, imploring his aid and that of the British navy. Spotswood agreed to help and promised to send a raiding party composed of men from two British warships then in Virginia ports.

And so it came about that, in November 1718, Blackbeard was at anchor at Ocracoke near the spot called Blackbeard's or Teach's Hole. He was expecting no trouble, but he had his full crew aboard, and the *Adventure* was repaired and in good shape for the sea.

Unknown to the pirates, two sloops under the command of Lieutenant Maynard had arrived late the night before. Sent, as promised by Governor Spotswood, to search for the pirates, these ships were manned by British sailors and marines from the British navy. They were under orders to take the brigand Blackbeard dead or alive. This they intended to do.

At dawn on that clear, cold November day, Lieutenant Maynard sent out two small skiffs to take soundings to try to find the depth of the water near the anchored *Adventure*. If possible, they were to find a deep-water access to the pirate craft. These strange and suspicious-looking craft were fired on by the *Adventure* when they failed to answer a hail. The accurate small-arms fire from the *Adventure* was intended to warn rather than to harm, but it drove the skiffs back to their parent ship in a hurry.

At this point, the British ensign was run up on both sloops, and Blackbeard's hail was answered by a volley of rifle fire as the smaller of the two sloops set her sails and tried to find a channel through the sand bars to engage the *Adventure.* The channel was as tricky then as it is now, and the Britisher ran hard aground and stuck fast. This greatly delighted Teach, who knew these waters as most men know their dooryards. This stranded smaller sloop would be easy prey after he had dealt with the larger vessel, he thought.

That larger sloop, the *Ranger*, was under the personal command of Maynard, who immediately got her under way and sailed closer to Blackbeard to make his small-arms fire more effective. To Blackbeard's great glee, the *Ranger* also ran aground, but what appeared to be a more-or-less permanent stranding turned out in a few moments to have been only a temporary disabling of Maynard's vessel. Thinking he now had the *Ranger* at his mercy, Blackbeard slipped his anchor cable and left the secure position he had held behind the sand reef. Under a favorable wind and keeping to the familiar channel, he ran straight for the *Ranger.*

At Teach's bellowed order, the gun-ports were opened on both sides of the *Adventure*, and the cannon were run out, so that their muzzles protruded beyond the sides of the ship. Charges and load were placed in each cannon, and matches were made ready. Down bore the pirate ship upon the *Ranger.* At the last moment before collision, she turned alongside and brought her starboard guns to bear. The cannon fired almost as one, raking the *Ranger* fore and aft. As the *Adventure* then wheeled to return and present her larboard battery, Maynard hastily ordered his men below decks. Around came the buccaneer and sailed smartly back. This time the larboard cannon fired, again sweeping the decks of the *Ranger* fore and aft. However, this time there were no casualties since only the dead from the previous salvo had remained on deck with Maynard.

Seeing an apparently helpless sloop at his mercy, Teach then gave the order to come alongside and board the *Ranger*. Even as the grappling irons were being thrown, however, Maynard called to his men below decks, and they swarmed back topside, armed to the teeth with pistols and swords.

As was his custom, Teach led the screaming, howling charge of men from one craft to the other. Cutlass and pistol in hand, he sprang to the deck of the *Ranger* and immediately sought out her commanding officer. For one brief instant in eternity Blackbeard and Maynard glared into each other's eyes. Then, with a curse, Blackbeard charged, only to be met by the pointblank fire from Maynard's pistol. Tearing a groove along the side of the pirate's head, the bullet grazed but did not kill him. With a roar of pain and anger, Teach sprang once again for his adversary; but this time one of Maynard's sword-wielding marines attacked from the side. Swinging the heavy blade down with both hands and with all his might, the marine cut so deeply into the side of Blackbeard's neck that it seemed he almost severed the great head from its body.

With blood spouting from this gigantic cut and gore from his head wound almost blinding him, our pirate, nonetheless, closed with Maynard in an attempt to kill him as, all around them, the boarding party fought desperately with the Britishers. Maynard was too skillful a swordsman to be pinned down, and he fenced with Blackbeard, eluding him, dodging, and inflicting yet more wounds on the huge body. The magnificent beard was now covered with matted blood, and the cruel eyes were beginning to glaze. Finally, Teach drew back one step, raised his pistol with his left hand to blast his enemy, and fell forward on his face, quite dead, the smouldering match still around his head and almost touching the boots of Lieutenant Maynard. When they examined the body later, it was found that Teach had sustained some thirty-seven major wounds, including that deadly cut in his neck, any one of which would have stopped a lesser man.

Seeing their leader fall, the pirates then jumped into Pamlico Sound and swam or waded ashore. Their liberty was short lived, however, since they were all rounded up and taken back to Virginia for trial. All but Israel Hands and one other were convicted of piracy and treason and hanged. Hands turned state's evidence and escaped the death penalty.

When Blackbeard had been killed, his head was cut off and affixed to the bowsprit of the *Ranger*. There it remained until the ship returned to Virginia. What was finally done with the grisly trophy is not recorded, but there is one fine family in Massachusetts which claims that the skull was made into a giant cup, was then silver-plated, and is now in their possession. The great, mutilated body of Blackbeard was tossed unceremoniously overboard where, legend claims, it swam three times around the entangled *Ranger* and *Adventure* before it sank from sight beneath the water.

Israel Hands, Blackbeard's crippled first mate, returned to England after the piracy trial and lived out his life in London. Governor Spotswood, however, although his term of governor had expired, steadfastly refused to return to England. He gave as his reason his fear of what other pirates might do to him—the man who had been responsible for the death of the famous Blackbeard—if they could manage to capture him. Thus did the fear generated by Blackbeard actually outlive the man himself.

Many men have tried to discover the fabled treasure that

Blackbeard admitted having buried. Legend has it that Teach traveled as far inland as the site of the present town of Grimesland, some ten miles east of Greenville, North Carolina, on the Tar River. At this location the pirate is said to have had a sister, who lived on a small farm which he had bought for her and which, in fact, still bears her name in the ancient records of the county. Blackbeard is said to have visited her on several occasions to recuperate from wounds and from extended sprees. There is an extremely old cypress tree near this site. With its roots in the waters of the river, it towers above all the other trees in the area. This tree is called "Old Table-Top" and was used as a lookout where the brigand stationed one of his henchmen to keep watch down the river and to warn against sudden attack. The tree is, indeed, flat across the top, and it would be a comparatively easy matter to construct a platform there which would command a view of the Tar River almost to the town of Washington. Great excitement prevailed in the neighborhood in 1933 when a Mr. Lee dug out of the river bank nearby a small iron pot half-filled with old silver coins of various sizes.

Blount's Creek near Washington, North Carolina, is another location where the treasure has been hunted and dug for, as well as Holliday's Island near the town of Edenton. If any of the searchers found any treasure, they have kept the secret well. A farmer did plow up a metal bucket near Bath and found therein a number of silver coins and three gold coins, all of foreign make and all very old, but these were never definitely tied to Teach, and it is thought that perhaps some settler fearful of an Indian attack buried them there.

To this day at Ocracoke some will tell you that the "Teach lights" are still seen on occasion both over and in the waters of Pamlico Sound. Blackbeard's ghostly ship is sometimes seen in the light of the waning moon. Some say the headless figure of

Blackbeard can be seen in the dark of the moon as it swims around and around Teach's Hole, searching for its severed head. They aver that it gleams with a phosphorescent glow and is plainly visible just below the surface of the water.

When Teach's lights are seen, either above or below the surface of the water, it always portends disaster of some sort for the ones who see them. If there be a man brave or foolish enough to follow those lights until they come to rest, he would find Blackbeard's buried treasure. The only trouble is, he would also find the devil himself, sitting cross-legged on the treasure claiming his half as Blackbeard's sworn partner.

The Ghostly Hornpipe

from *Blackbeard's Cup and Stories of the Outer Banks*

Once isolated and accessible only with difficulty, the charming village of Ocracoke is now known to most Carolina vacationers if only as a prime spot for a summer holiday. There time does, indeed, sometimes seem to stand still. Not so familiar is what has been preserved in the Town of Portsmouth, just across Ocracoke Inlet from the village. Now only a memory, Portsmouth was at one time a very important port of entry for ocean-going commerce.

The region was already growing steadily at the beginning of the eighteenth century. Hatteras Inlet to the north was shoaling up, and more and more sea traffic began to use Portsmouth. Ocracoke Inlet, then as now, was very tricky and changeable and a local pilot was needed to bring an incoming vessel past the sand bars and shoals. For this reason there grew up a straggling tent city near the present site of Ocracoke Village which was populated by professional pilots who knew the inlet well.

They located here to be on the lookout night and day for incoming merchant ships needing a local pilot. Portsmouth was the destination of these vessels, and the wharves and docks, chandleries and saloons and stores of that city welcomed the weary seamen. "Pilot City," later to become Ocracoke Village, was temporary lodging for the pilots. Most of them maintained homes in or near Portsmouth.

Fishing was also an important industry, and the nearby Gulf Stream and adjacent waters usually provided abundant catches of very marketable fish. Even the inedible menhaden, still known locally as "fatback," was much in demand in the fall and early summer. Farmers, planting their successive crops of corn, followed the ancient practice of the friendly Indians from whom they first learned about this exclusively American grain. From the beginning, the Indians planted a raw fish in each hill of corn, along with four grains of seed. An Indian legend revolved around this practice, and today we realize that this timeless method provided the corn with excellent fertilizer. Thence came the colonial rhyme that the farmer often repeated as he dropped the four grains in the hill: "One for the raven and one for the crow, one to rot and one to grow."

One of the most successful commercial fishermen of Portsmouth Town was a man named Jesse Hawkins. He was very energetic and resourceful and was usually among the leaders of these farmers of the sea. He was economical almost to the point of stinginess and was an expert at "making do" with equipment long after most seafarers would have replaced it with new.

A typical example was his schooner, the *Taurus*, which he had purchased in Charleston some years before from the widow of a fisherman. Well built, she was admirably suited for the task of offshore fishing but most of her equipment was already old when Hawkins bought her. Her standing rigging was frayed in places and her suit of sails had seen better days. Her anchor cable was an ancient hemp hawser, thick as a man's thigh. It looked strong enough to anchor a continent, but it had held through many a gale and now groaned whenever even a moderate amount of strain was put on the anchor. Her ribs seemed sound, however, and her holds were of ample size to contain large hauls of fish. She was put to use almost the year round as her catches followed the changing seasons. Although he was known as a sometimes reckless skipper, Hawkins had little difficulty in obtaining a competent crew. He was known to be a fair man, if a hard driver, and his crews usually prospered as he prospered.

Competition among the fishing vessels was intense but friendly. Most of the fishing was done on "shares," as the captain and the crew shared the proceeds from whatever catch they made. Although the captain was in full command, the crew had a vested interest in the success or failure of each trip. Often the difference between a highly successful voyage and a commonplace one was the luck or the hustle of getting to the offshore fishing grounds early. The more successful skippers put to sea in the late afternoon and anchored overnight on the edge of the best fishing spots to await the daylight.

Thus it was that on the first night of the full moon in November 1714, the schooner *Taurus* was anchored just inside the Outer Slough waiting for the first light of day to begin what they hoped should be, by all the signs and portents, a very successful fishing trip. Several hundred yards to the south of the schooner the sloop *Goodfortune* rode easily to her anchor in the increasing swells. Much smaller than the *Taurus* but much newer and more nimble, she was captained by young Arthur Newby, another of the more able fishermen of Portsmouth. He, too, had gone out early to be on hand near the best fishing spots when the expected heavy run of fish began. The crews of each vessel could see the lights of the other as they rose and fell with the motion of the sea.

It is strange, indeed, that neither of the captains noticed the steady falling of the glass, as the barometers were called. Both were accustomed to the frequent, sudden changes in the weather at this time of year but perhaps they were both preoccupied. Even so, the growing size of the waves which now began to break over the shoals should have alerted them to the fact that something was up weatherwise. Maybe they anticipated only a brief squall which they could handle with ease.

One by one the stars were blotted out by the incoming line of clouds and the moon itself grew dimmer and dimmer and finally was completely obscured by the cloud bank. No lights whatsoever were visible in the blackness except for the anchor lights of the two vessels and an occasional wave of phosphorescent fire in the depths of the sea. The wind song slowly changed from a low moan to a higher and higher pitched scream as the full force of the winter storm struck.

All hands were called up on deck on both vessels as the experienced seamen sought to secure all loose gear and ready their craft for the full impact of the blow. It was not long in coming. Line squalls are infamous for the brute force of their initial attack, and this one was unusually fierce even for November in this graveyard of ships. Both captains elected to stay at anchor rather than cut loose and run before the storm. As the seas grew higher and higher, both craft jerked more and more forcibly against their anchors and even experienced sailors were thrown to the deck. Both vessels were securely anchored and both tried to pay out a bit more anchor cable to ease the snatching caused by the waves.

Suddenly, and with an ear-splitting crack, the anchor cable

of the *Taurus* parted under the strain and the large schooner was at the mercy of the wind and surf. "Release the jib!" roared Captain Hawkins, and his crew sprang to unfurl this foremost of the sails to gain some control. The jib sail filled and bellied out in the gale all right and was beginning to bring the bow of the ship downwind but in the next instant it split wide open with a sound like that of a cannon firing. The foresail suffered the same fate, as the old canvas could not withstand the full force of the storm. *Taurus* was a derelict out of control and directly upwind now from the anchored *Goodfortune*.

Captain Hawkins could do nothing at this point to control his vessel as she bore down, headlong, upon the smaller *Goodfortune*. Seeing the danger, Captain Newby cast off from his anchor and was beginning to turn his vessel around, but in the instant that she was broadside the *Taurus*, the larger schooner struck her amidships and rolled her over and over under its keel, cutting her almost in two and sinking her with all hands. Hawkins threw overboard all his life preservers and some of his hatch covers in the faint hope that some members of the crew could be saved, but it was to no avail.

Taurus brought up on a sand bar off a lee shore on the southern end of Portsmouth Island. She was easily refloated two days later with no loss of life. Under a jury rig, she limped back into Portsmouth harbor and was later repaired and refitted at the ship's chandlery there. Some of the wreckage of the *Goodfortune* washed up on the southern shore of the island, but no bodies were ever recovered.

As the details of the wreck spread through the port, there was some muttering among the seaman against Captain Hawkins.

"'E shouda reploiced that anchor cable long ago," some said.

"'E's to bloime for the drowndin' of them poor lads and 'e's the one what sent 'em to their deaths unshriven and unburied to roll about the bottom o' the sea 'till kingdom come. 'E ought to be brought to account," others whispered. "Poor dears, they'll never rest."

Most of the townfolk defended the captain. No one could know that the great cable would fail. After all, they argued, he was an experienced captain and surely he would not have placed his own life in danger if he had ever dreamed that such a thing could happen. Time went by. The *Taurus* was refitted with all new cordage and a brand-new suit of sails and the day came when she was ready to put to sea again. Captain Hawkins had visited all the families of the dead crewmen and expressed his sorrow at the tragedy. The families were used to danger and to tragedy on the sea, and they reassured him that they in no way held him to blame.

Well, the schooner was ready and Captain Hawkins was ready, and so plans were made to return to the business of fishing to try to recoup the heavy expense of refitting the vessel. He had not the slightest difficulty in recruiting the same crew of experienced seamen who had sailed with him before. Late one sunny afternoon they put out again through Ocracoke Inlet and out to sea. Once again they anchored near the same spot as before to wait for the first light of day. They all agreed it was an excellent place to begin a day's fishing. In the murky light just before dawn, they set their nets and marked the place with net buoys. The sea seemed to be alive with fish and they anticipated sharing in a near record catch. All day long they left those nets in place and, as the sunny afternoon turned into the early darkness of November, they prepared to haul them in.

Prepared is all they did. As they began to haul in the line attached to the net, the whole sea and the deck of their ship was suddenly bathed in a mysterious, greenish light. There, in that ghostly light on the deck, they beheld to their horror the spirits of the dead seamen from the little *Goodfortune*! Without a word, the ghosts began to haul in the nets and dump the catch into the hold of the schooner. With precision they performed all duties that go with bringing such nets aboard and emptying them. All the laboring fishermen had obviously drowned—they had wet hair streaming down to their waists, gaping mouths, and sightless, staring eyes. They made no sound but each ghost went about his task with the sureness and skill of much experience. They worked together to secure the catch like the well-trained team they were. The crew of the *Taurus* could only cower against the masts and the cabin and stare at this apparition with wild and frantic eyes. Many repeatedly crossed themselves and pleaded aloud for divine protection.

As the last bight of the net was emptied into the hold, there came a brilliant flash of blue-green light and then utter darkness and silence except for the gentle swish of the seas running alongside the ship. The ghosts of the drowned seamen vanished as quickly as they had come. A trembling Captain Hawkins gave the orders to bring his vessel about. In silence he conned her through the inlet and to the dockside in Portsmouth. Once safely docked, he got a lighted lantern and went down into the hold of his ship to estimate his catch. There was not one single fish in the craft! Not one fish of any kind! The hold of the *Taurus* was as empty as when he had set out on this venture. Some of the crew crowded down into the hold behind him and cried out in disbelief and wonder. The nets were strewn about the deck but none of them was torn or in any way the worse for wear. There were no fish, but with their own eyes the crew had seen thousands of them dumped into the hold!

Captain Jesse Hawkins was able to obtain crews for just two more fishing trips offshore. The first crew was a full crew, although it contained none of his original personnel. The same thing happened, although they fished an entirely different area of ocean. The same ghostly group of men fished the nets with exactly the same results—nothing. The second crew was really about half a crew, just enough men to handle the schooner and several of them were drunk by the time they came aboard. No matter. The outcome was exactly the same and they made the trip back to the safety of the dock in record time.

After that, no one would sail with Captain Hawkins again. The *Taurus* stayed tied up to the wharf and gradually rotted away from neglect. She grew less and less seaworthy as shipwrights refused to work on her and prospective buyers would have none of her. Finally, she rotted away and sank at her moorings. No effort was ever made to salvage anything from her or to remove her. She was truly a landlocked derelict.

The haunted captain disappeared from Portsmouth Town and was never seen there again. Some say that he took up piracy as a crewman aboard one of the pirate raiders which began to become more numerous a short time later. Others claimed that he committed suicide and that, at his end, the devil was there to claim him. At any rate, he was never heard from again.

Not so the *Taurus*. There were people who swore that if you went to the spot where she had sunk on any moonlit midnight in the month of November, you could see a strange ghostly light illuminating her sunken decks. There, by that light, you would see a terrifying sight.

Back and forth upon the sodden and rotted decks, they say, the drowned fishermen of the *Goodfortune* dance a macabre dance, a sailor's hornpipe! Back and forth and round and round they dance in an intricate sort of quadrille which, for centuries, has been the sailor's dance. There is old Pegleg Henry with his accordian playing the tune. The leader of the hornpipe appears to be one-eyed Jack Austin with his black eye-patch. These and all the other departed comrades whom the people of Portsmouth Town had known so well. All the people who knew these departed fishermen are themselves dead now, and Portsmouth Town is but a ghost of its former busy, bustling self. Just a few structures have been preserved for posterity to see and admire.

Some people contend that the ghostly hornpipe continues to this day. They claim that if you can get the operator of a small boat to take you to the spot on any November night with a bright moon, you will be rewarded with a strange sight. Gaze down into the deep water where the *Taurus* finally went to rest and they aver that you will see the ghosts and watch their hornpipe. They say that this will continue until the day of judgment, when the souls of those poor drowned crewmen and their captain will receive the peace and rest they so desperately desire.

Hatteras Jack

from *Legends of the Outer Banks and Tar Heel Tidewater*

For as many years as there have been deep water sailors, man has been fascinated by and strangely drawn to porpoises. Long before the advent of the internal-combustion marine engine and while navigators were still in bondage to the vagaries of wind and current, a rather large body of half-truth and half-legend grew up about these playful and intelligent kings of the deep.

Australia, for example, boasted of a very unusual specimen, who (not which, mind you, but who) met the early sailing ships carrying the prisoner-colonists to new homes on that continent and led the ships safely into sheltered anchorage. Pelorus Jack, as this purposeful porpoise was called, is as much a part of Australian legend as is the jolly swagman and his jimbuck.

At about the same time or possibly a little later in history (the exact times are not very clear) the Outer Banks of North Carolina had a similar phenomenon. Whereas the Australian porpoise was the standard brown and black, the Hatteras version was almost snow-white, a rare albino specimen. Whereas Pelorus Jack apparently contented himself with meeting and guiding inbound vessels, Hatteras Jack was a more versatile performer and greatly endeared himself not only to the pilots of Hatteras-bound vessels but to the permanent residents of those parts as well. With the exception of the short-lived porpoise fishery on Portsmouth Island, which was conceived and operated by outlanders for a few short months with only a few native boatmen as employees, the love affair between porpoises and the Outer Bankers has continued to this day.

North Carolina's Outer Banks are pierced at intervals by inlets where the waters of the Atlantic Ocean and the coastal sounds meet. Since the first attempts to settle this country, seafaring men have used these inlets to gain access to the mainland.

Many of the inlets known to ancient mariners have gradually closed up, so that they no longer exist except as names on very old maps. Examples of these are Raleigh's Inlet, which is said to have been located about nine miles north of the present Oregon Inlet, and, more recently, Caffey's Inlet, which used to exist a few miles north of the town of Duck.

Other openings in the banks appear to have become fairly permanent either by the action of man in stabilizing them or by the relatively fixed set of the currents that sweep through them. Such are Beaufort Inlet, which served the Port of Morehead City, and Hatteras and Oregon Inlets to the north.

Even with the best efforts of man and the relative predictability of the permanent currents, most inlets are treacherous and dangerous to shipping unless a local pilot cons the helm to avoid the ever-shifting shoals and reefs. This is true even in this day of sonar, warning buoys, and flashing lights. It was true to an even greater degree in the days before these aids to navigation.

In the days of the pirate Blackbeard, Ocracoke Inlet was the customary gateway for ships wishing to come to safe anchor on the North Carolina coast. The town of Portsmouth was booming on the south shore of that inlet and was the trading center for the whole area. To the north lay Silver Lake, a safe and land-locked haven for the careening of ships. Later the majority of this traffic moved to Hatteras Inlet, some fifteen miles to the north, and this inlet remained the favorite for many years thereafter. It was here that the Confederate forts were built and here that the sea-born Yankee invasion of the Civil War took place. Between the Revolution and the Civil War, Hatteras Inlet handled the vast majority of the ships and shipping trade for most of eastern Carolina.

This inlet, closest to the "Graveyard of the Atlantic," was then and remains today one of the most difficult to navigate. The topography of the sea and inlet bottom are constantly changing, and what may be a deep channel today can well be a dangerous reef next week. Most ships need deep water to stay afloat, at least deeper than the two or three feet over these ever-moving shoals and reefs. Deep water there is in Hatteras Inlet, but it is confined to a twisting, turning, and ever-changing channel. Snakelike it is in its complicated convolutions and continuous motion.

Imagine, if you can, the dilemma of those ante-bellum captains. With no auxiliary motor and only the power of the wind to propel them, they would creep with shortened sail into this inlet. With a sailor stationed in the chains, constantly heaving the lead line and calling out the decreasing depth, and with a lookout at the masthead, pointing out the breakers ahead, it is remarkable that any skipper would even attempt the passage.

It was about the year 1790 that help arrived upon the scene in the "person" of Hatteras Jack. Now, according to the tales that Hatterasmen tell when the winter winds are howling and they are sitting snug ashore around their warm stoves, Hatteras Jack was just as real as Edward Teach and a sight more helpful. While other porpoises contented themselves with sporting about the breakers and being mistaken for mermaids, Jack had a purpose in life.

That self-imposed duty, that high calling to which he was devoted, was the leading of ships into and out of Hatteras Inlet. He was the self-appointed pilot, and he never lost a ship during all of his long career. Captains of inbound ships would lie to off the inlet or else track back and forth and wait for Hatteras Jack to put in an appearance. With the coming of high tide, there he would be, leaping clear of the water and swimming in figure-eights, his friendly grin just awash in the blue-green waters.

With a single prolonged blast on the ship's fog horn and an answering series of high-pitched squeaks from Jack, the piloting would begin. Slowly, now, so that the sailing boat would have no trouble in keeping up, Jack would head into the channel. Slowly he would swim through the various twists and turns of the channel-of-the-day, his white back gleaming just under the surface and the sailing vessel following in his wake. Carefully keeping to the very center of the deep water, Hatteras Jack would lead the vessel past the shoals, past the reefs, around the fishhook-shaped tip of Hatteras Island, and into the relatively safe waters of the Sound.

Once the escorted ship had come to rest and had let go her anchors with a roar of unwinding chain, the albino porpoise would go into a transport of glee, apparently at having concluded another successful mission. Unless there was another ship awaiting him outside the bar, he would then proceed to put on a show of tail-walking on the surface of the water, of complicated leaps and flips into the air, and of swift dartings and barrel-rolls just under the surface.

Hatteras Jack never sought, and apparently did not expect, any sort of reward from his human friends for services rendered. About the only reward he would have been interested in anyway, it was said, would have been a fish or two, but he was a much more accomplished fisherman than any human. The satisfaction of a job well done and the rendering of aid that only he could give are believed to have been the motivating reasons for his work. There are many things that man does not yet understand about porpoises. The instances of help that have been given man by this most intelligent of marine animals are legion and as yet not fully explained.

The story goes that our albino porpoise would carefully appraise each ship before undertaking the responsibility of guiding her into the inlet. If a ship appeared to be larger or more heavily laden than usual and thus deeper in the water, it is said that Hatteras Jack would literally take her measurements by diving on her port side, traversing the outline of her hull under water, and then surfacing on her starboard side. Thus, having sensed her draft and knowing well the depth of the water in the channel, he would know just how full the tide must be for that particular vessel to make a safe trip through the tricky channel.

No matter how many blasts were sounded on the fog horn, our guiding porpoise would steadfastly refuse to begin the trip until the tide had risen to a safe depth. While awaiting that hour, it is said, he would normally put on a show for the crew of the waiting ship. Sometimes alone and sometimes in company with other porpoises, he would exhibit the tremendous agility that porpoises possess and the keen sense of humor they are known to have. There were times, too, when he would engage in fights to the death with his mortal enemy, the shark. These combats were as spectacular as they were terrifying. Almost as much of the combat took place just above the surface of the water as occurred beneath it. The superior speed and intelligence of Hatters Jack always brought him out the victor, and although the shark had terrible teeth and a savage will to fight, he was just no match for the porpoise.

This, then, is the story of Hatteras Jack—pilot, entertainer, warrior, and friend to man. This is the legend that has been handed down from generation to generation. This, plus the Outer Bankers' own happy experiences and encounters with present-day porpoises, is the reason why no real Outer Banker, native or adopted, will harm these creatures or permit them to be harmed if such harm can be prevented.

Call them bottle-nosed dolphins if you like; they are not fish, but mammals, which (or who) breathe air as we do, bear their young alive and nurse them at the breast, talk with each other in their own language, and have their own highly organized communities with laws which are rigidly obeyed. The brain of this remarkable animal is just as convoluted and complex as is the brain of man, and it is a great deal larger. One wonders what might have happened if the porpoise had had the advantage of an opposable thumb—but maybe he is much happier and better off as he is.

After bouys, lights, and bells or horns were put on platforms out in the inlet to mark the channel, Hatteras Jack just disappeared. He came back, they say, a time or two afterwards, as though he were checking all this newfangled equipment to see if it was really effective. He actually led a boat through the channel once in a while as though to keep his "fin in." His visits grew less frequent, however, and he finally stopped coming at all, but many still remember him and speak of him with love and gratitude. He is part and parcel of their tradition. He, too, was a real Outer Banker.

Sea-born Woman

from *The Flaming Ship of Ocracoke & Other Tales of the Outer Banks*

The year was 1720, and the month was the often stormy September. The Irish emigrant ship, *Celestial Harp*, had made heavy weather of the voyage since leaving Belfast several weeks before. Head winds and stormy seas had made the trip a succession of miserable days and restbroken nights for the poor emigrants huddled below decks. The stench from the whale-oil lamps swinging from the low ceiling mixed with the human odors inevitable in such close confinement. The sickening roll and pitch of the ship distressed many an already queasy stomach, and the pitiful passengers were a sorry-looking lot indeed.

Most of them had worked long and hard, had scrimped and saved to accumulate passage money for this trip. Conditions were almost intolerably hard for the poor in Ireland at that time, and the dream of a life in that New World across the sea seemed, to many, like the hope of a Promised Land, a land of opportunity and of beginning again. This was the dream that sustained them. This was the vision that, even now, was stronger than the fear of sudden shipwreck and death in the stormy North Atlantic.

John and Mary O'Hagan considered themselves to be more fortunate than most of the emigrants. John had his skill in carpentry, which was sure to be much in demand in the new country, and Mary had the frugality and good common sense of the typical Irish housewife. More than that, Mary was expecting the birth of their first child any day now, and thank God, there were two midwives in the company, thus assuring her the very best of care. The O'Hagans considered themselves to be greatly blessed.

Two days earlier the weather had cleared, and, as if an omen of brighter days to come, the wind had abated and hauled favorably and the seas had subsided. At long last, the emigrants were able to come out on deck and enjoy the sights, sounds, and fresh smells of a brisk day at sea. Their joy was complete when the Captain told them that the worst weather was now past and that they were almost within sight of Massachusetts Colony, where they could expect to land within the week.

Just over the horizon, some twenty or thirty miles to the southward, another group of seafarers was also rejoicing over the improvement in the weather. The flotilla of five pirate ships under the command of the famous buccaneer captain, Edward Low, had had very poor hunting, and the motley crews were eager and fretting for action. Discipline had become more of a problem than ever among the cutthroat sailors, and there had even been rumblings of a possible mutiny and a departure to warmer climes and better hunting grounds.

The pirates had come north hoping to intercept merchant ships loaded with valuable cargoes but, so far, had encountered only the huge, crashing, green seas of the North Atlantic. The gale-force winds had blown almost incessantly, and never a potential quarry had come into view, although many could have slipped past undetected in the driving rain and mist. The sudden break in the weather and the reappearance of the sun brightened the spirits of the sea rovers, and they were literally spoiling for action.

This mission had been undertaken jointly by the five ships, so when the weather improved, Captain Low called a hurried conference of his captains on the afterdeck of his ship. There it was decided that three of the five vessels would sail in various southerly directions in search of prey. Low's ship and the *Delight*, captained by Low's favorite subordinate, Francis Carrington Spriggs, would sail in still other directions towards the north. Rendezvous was set for six months later at New Providence, which at that time served as one of the major pirate capitals of the world.

Just before first light the next morning, Spriggs and his crew of eighteen weighed anchor on the *Delight*, eased the ship away from Low's ship, and made full sail northward in the darkness. As the *Delight* squared away on her new course and left the other ships behind, Captain Spriggs himself raised his new flag swiftly to the main truck, the highest point on the vessel. The crew cheered lustily at the sight of this sinister symbol of piracy, several broke into a clumsy sort of hornpipe dance. The young captain had designed the flag to suit his own particular taste, and it was unique in the pirate world. It consisted of a large rectangular piece of black cloth on which was sewn the figure of a white skeleton holding an hourglass in one bony hand and an arrow on which was impaled a bleeding heart in the other hand. The flag snapped in the fresh, early morning breeze as though it had a life of its own.

Northward then drove the *Delight* and her newly independent captain. A fresh breeze poured over her port quarter, and her damp sails were set and drawing well. Northward she sped and, as fate would have it, on a course which would intercept that of the plodding *Celestial Harp* and her human cargo.

It was about first light the next morning when the lookout in the main shrouds of the pirate ship cried his sighting of the emigrant vessel. By midday the two ships lay alongside each other and the brief resistance on the part of the crew of the *Celestial Harp* had ended. The shipload of pitiful passengers were now all pirate captives and in very real danger of immediate and violent death.

Captain Spriggs' disappointment at the poverty of his prize can be imagined. The captured ship, herself, was too slow and clumsy to be worth confiscating, and the few supplies she had left were hardly worth transferring to his own craft. The anger of the pirate skipper was an evil token for his captives. Even for one so young, Captain Spriggs was already building a reputation, not only for bravery, but for cruelty, for it was his habit to put to death all captured seamen so that they might not later testify against him. "Dead men tell no tales," he had cried on more than one occasion such as this, and he was prepared to practice his philosophy now.

Maybe it was because of his disappointment or maybe it was just to impress his crew that he now devised a new and more dramatic way to forever close the mouths of his captives. Pirate crews were always notoriously close to mutiny, and an example of savagery was usually helpful in keeping them in their place. Whatever the reason, the method of extermination, this time, was to be most unusual.

Personally supervising his crew, Spriggs ordered kegs of gunpowder secured at strategic places near the waterline of the emigrant ship. Fuses of varying lengths were then run from these powder kegs to a central spot on the deck. According to the pirate's calculations, if he lighted the fuses at one-minute intervals, he would have time to get off the doomed ship and, then, all the powder kegs would explode simultaneously, blowing the ship to bits. The men of the *Celestial Harp*, passengers and crew alike, were chained to masts and stanchions so that they could neither interfere with the grand explosion nor leap into the sea to save themselves. The careful planning and preparation was all accomplished before the terrified eyes of the chained men, whose pleading and prayers the pirates scornfully ignored. This was to be a blast that would live in pirate history.

Meanwhile, below the foredeck and completely unknown to the pirates, another drama was taking place. The two midwives, working in frantic haste, were preparing for the birth of Mary O'Hagan's child. Whether or not the excitement and despair caused by the pirate invasion had hastened the event, there was now no time to consider, nor did it matter. The greatest of God's recurring miracles was about to take place, and the three women most immediately concerned would not be bothered with what was going on above decks, even though death itself might be imminent. A baby was about to be born.

Thus was Mary O'Hagan delivered of a beautiful, large baby girl in the dim light of swinging oil lamps in the stuffy hold of a ship which was hove to and rolling restlessly in the waves. A delighted smile creased the face of the elder midwife as she held the new-born child up by the ankles and slapped her smartly with an open hand across the little buttocks. The sound of the first healthy wail from the baby's lungs echoed and reechoed in the confines of the hold, penetrated the hatch openings, and sounded on the deck of the *Celestial Harp*, where men stood ready to torture and kill upon their leader's signal.

What prompted Captain Francis Spriggs' next move is

known only to God. It could have been that he felt some stirring of pity for his helpless victims after his first anger at their poverty had passed. It could have been that he suddenly remembered an ancient superstition of pirates that it is very lucky for a new captain to release his first prize, just as some fishermen always throw back the first fish caught. It is quite possible that he quickly realized that the blessed event provided him with a means of saving face before his crew, while making his offering on the altar of luck at the same time. Whatever the reason, he reacted immediately.

Beaming with honest joy when he was told of the birth, he sent below to inquire if the new-born baby was a boy or a girl. Upon learning that the child was a girl, he fairly capered with delight. He pointed again and again, first to the name board of his own ship where the title *Delight* appeared in foot-high gilt letters, then back to the hatchway from whence came the lusty cries of the baby. He seemed to sense some connection between the ship's name and the arrival of the child, and the coincidence pleased him beyond measure.

Summoning the master of the emigrant ship, the first mate, and the baby's father John O'Hagan, the pirate chieftain made them a proposition. "Only name the baby girl for my dear old mother," he said, "and I'll let your ship go free. Call her Jerushia—Jerushia Spriggs O'Hagan—and you can all go with my blessing."

Well, it didn't take them long to accept such a one-sided choice as that, and so the bargain was made. The gunpowder kegs and unlit fuses were removed from the *Celestial Harp* as the baby's name was entered in the ship's log as Jerushia Spriggs O'Hagan. Both John and Mary O'Hagan signed the book in agreement to the name, and it was duly witnessed by both midwives, the Captain, and the first mate.

So pleased was Captain Spriggs with the acceptance of his offer that he immediately sent a small boat back to the *Delight* to fetch a bolt of cloth-of-gold, which he gave to Mary O'Hagan with the strict admonition that it be used only to make a wedding gown for Jerushia when she was grown to womanhood and had chosen her man.

On this note, the two ships parted. The *Celestial Harp* plowed, once again, on her way to Massachusetts, and the *Delight* headed southward, her cannon booming out a long, rolling salute of twelve guns as the distance widened between the vessels.

In the New World, John O'Hagan's skills with the drawing knife, the saw, and the chisel stood him in good stead. Settling in New Bedford, he developed into one of the finest shipbuilders available, and his services were much in demand. As he worked and prospered, little Jerushia grew and developed until the fame of her Irish beauty spread far and wide. The sea baby had become beautiful on a majestic scale. A full six feet tall she was, slender and graceful. To set off her willowy figure, she was blessed with hair the color of mahogany, which fell like a cape to her waist. With lovely, regular features and an open, sunny disposition, she was the favorite of young and old. Only one incident marred those golden years. When she was twelve, Jerushia's mother died, and the duties of the household fell on her young shoulders.

All during those happy years, there was never a Christmas which passed without a very special gift from Captain Spriggs, and, on each birthday, he sent her a bolt of very fine cloth of some description from which she delighted in making her own special dresses. The pirate had searched out the whereabouts of the girl he had spared and took pleasure in remembering her special days. Jerushia called him "Godfather," although she actually saw him only a very few times during those years.

In due time, she chose from among her many suitors a young sea captain. She was married in New Bedford, in a dress of Captain Spriggs' cloth-of-gold. The union was blessed with three children, all boys. It was, indeed, a happy period in Jerushia's life, a time of loving and sharing, of growth and blessed contentment.

What happened to Captain Francis Spriggs for several years after that September day in 1720, when he sailed away from the reprieved *Celestial Harp*, is not clear. It is almost certain that he did sail back to the pirate rendezvous at New Providence, for if he had not, his fellow pirates would have hunted him down and murdered him for breaking faith with the Brotherhood of the Sea, as they called themselves. Apparently, his career as a pirate did not last very long, however. According to British Navy records, he met his first, and only, defeat fairly soon after the *Celestial Harp* incident. While plundering the Bay of Honduras, Spriggs and his crew were surprised by a British war ship. The *Delight* was run aground, and Spriggs and his ruffians escaped to shore.

There are no more official accounts of his pirating and, so far as the records of the British Admiralty show, he just dropped out of sight. There is no evidence that he ever took the King's Pardon, as so many of the Brotherhood who wanted to come ashore and live as honest men did. Neither is there any record that he thereafter engaged in any unlawful activity. His faithful remembering of Jerushia's birthdays and Christmases provides the only record of him for many years.

But, in 1741, Spriggs again surfaced on the sea of history as we catch a glimpse of him in Yorktown, Virginia. Here he was a ship owner and merchant of considerable means, owning several vessels engaged in trade with foreign countries. There is a record of his business and an account of his marriage and the death of his bride in less than a year in one of the terrible epidemics of those times. Still later it is known that he moved to Beaufort Town, sometimes called Hongry Town in that era, for a few years.

Meanwhile, the shadow of tragedy had fallen on Jerushia. Her father was killed in a shipyard accident, and, in a terrible storm in 1758, her husband and her youngest son were lost at sea. Her oldest son had become a preacher and went to live as a missionary among the Indians of the western plains. Her second son took over a portion of his father's business, but he married a woman as different from his mother as can be imagined. There always seemed to be some difference, some misunderstanding, between the two women, and Jerushia, while adequately provided for, lived a very lonely life. There was not much a widow could do in New Bedford in those days and, to make things worse, the business began to suffer reverses. Soon Jerushia was reduced to very modest circumstances and, at times, she felt the pinch of actual want.

This was the atmosphere when, in September of that year, her birthday came around and, for the very first time, no delivery van brought the customary bolt of cloth to her door. Already depressed, she broke down and cried miserably. Later that afternoon, she answered the bell at her door and saw, standing before her, a figure that was at once familiar and unfamiliar.

Her caller was a tall, erect man in his early sixties with graying hair and deeply tanned, but young-looking, skin. Some little thing, some mannerism of his as he removed his hat with a flourish and smiled at her, served to trigger her memory. With a rush of happiness, she recognized "Godfather Spriggs" and, like a little girl, threw her arms around his neck in welcome.

What a time those two must have had reminiscing on that day! The bolt of cloth was not missing; Francis Spriggs had brought it with him. He was in New Bedford on business, he told her, and must leave within the week. She told him of her loneliness, and he called on the young woman daily while he was there, telling her of his plans and his problems.

Having accumulated a great deal of wealth, he planned to retire from the world of business, for he wanted nothing more from life than to spend his remaining years somewhere near the sea, where he could read and perhaps tend a little garden and listen to the talk of seafaring men. He had purchased a plot of ground in a North Carolina town called Portsmouth, which was just south of Ocracoke Inlet and just across that inlet from Pilot Town, as some people called the village of Ocracoke. The Colony of Carolina was developing this town, and it was to be the biggest seaport anywhere around, with wharves and warehouses and shipfitting basins. There were many stores and shops and even plans for a large hospital to be located there. He had bought his plot at a reasonable price from his old friend, Colonel Michael Coutanch of Bath Town, and was even now building a two-story house with all the most modern conveniences known to the building trade.

Knowing Jerushia's loneliness, he asked her to move to Portsmouth as his housekeeper. In return, he offered her an excellent salary, considerate treatment, and the promise of the house itself at his death. Jerushia accepted the offer gladly, and thus began another of the happiest periods of her life.

Housekeeper she was, indeed, but Captain Spriggs, from the very first, treated her more like a daughter than a servant. Old enough to be her father and without children of his own, he lavished on her all the comforts he would have given to his own children. Jerushia had to plan the meals and buy provisions in the village of Portsmouth, but Spriggs provided her with a cook and a maid to do the heavy cleaning. Knowing her love of horses, he bought her a matched pair of black Arabians and a shiny black buggy to ride in. What a beautiful sight it must have been to see this tall, lovely woman, dressed all in widow's black but with a wealth of dark red hair streaming out behind her, as she drove her horses at full speed down the one road that extended the length of Portsmouth Island or walked them into Portsmouth Town to shop for groceries.

As Captain Spriggs had promised, "Spriggs' Luck," as the house was called, had all the conveniences known in that day. The ground floor was comprised of a large parlor and an equally large dining room. Off to one side was a sitting room and, on the other, a combination library-office, where the Captain handled the details of the shipping business in which he was still engaged. It was here that he also entertained his infrequent business visitors.

The second story contained four large bedrooms, and, out back, a dogtrot (now called a breezeway) connected the house with the kitchen and pantry, which were built separate from the main structure in order to protect the main house from the hazard of fire and the odors of cooking. The "necessary house" was a rather commodius two-room structure built some fifty or sixty feet to the rear of the kitchen and reached via a roofed, brick walkway extending from the back door of the kitchen. Thus it was entirely possible to walk, during a pouring rainstorm, from the main house through the dogtrot and the kitchen to the necessary house without once feeling a drop of rain or setting foot on the bare ground.

Spriggs' Luck had one macabre feature. In the large parlor there was a huge fireplace, complete with andirons and an iron cooking hook. The hearthstone in front of this opening was a large slab of solid marble some six inches thick, which served also as the lid for a concrete burial vault located immediately underneath. It was Spriggs' fancy that he wanted to be buried here so that his body would always be above the reach of the storm tides and still be part and parcel of the house that he loved so well. He had seen what those storms could, and sometimes would, do to an ordinary graveyard, and the thought haunted him. He made Jerushia promise that, should she outlive him, she would see that his burial was exactly as he wanted it.

Located well to the rear of the building was a small peach orchard with fifteen or twenty peach trees and a small pergola, or summerhouse, nestled in the center. Here the housekeeper could while away the afternoon hours of a spring day at reading or making lace, with the scent of the many bay trees and the peach blossoms heavy in the air and the muted sound of the surf in the middle distance. Off to one side were the carriage house and the stables where her blooded horses were kept.

Jerushia was far from selfish in her happiness. As though sensing in some way that she could not keep good fortune unless she shared it with the less happy, she became a veritable angel of mercy to the womenfolk of Portsmouth Town and Portsmouth Island. She trained herself to become as skillful as any midwife at the many duties surrounding childbirth, and her warm sympathy and ready wit made her a welcome assistant in times of stress and trouble. On her frequent trips by boat to New Berne and Beaufort and Edenton, she always inquired ahead of time what her neighbors would like brought to them. If she had to add a coin or two from her own purse to make up an unexpectedly high purchase price, no one was ever the wiser.

The unusual circumstances surrounding her birth soon became known to the island women, and, with the mysticism that comes so naturally to coastland folk, she became known simply as Sea-born Woman. As time passed, the people of Portsmouth grew to love her and rely on her and trust her.

So far as Jerushia knew, her benefactor did not have an enemy in world. The days of his piratical beginnings were long past and almost never mentioned. The days flowed by like a lazy stream, and Captain Spriggs seemed happy to live in Spriggs' Luck, taking part in an occasional fishing of the gill nets with friends from the village or conferring with an occasional visitor about some business manner. There were long, sunlit days in summer, too, when the Captain and his housekeeper would stroll the ocean beach of Portsmouth Island for miles. They would watch the many ships that used the port and wonder whence they came and whither they were bound.

Enemies he must have had, however, and they eventually searched him out and found him. Returning from the village late one afternoon in the winter of 1770, Jerushia wheeled her horses into the wide circle she usually described before entering the stables. As she approached the stable yard, both horses reared and shied in fright, so that it required all her strength to control them. In the fading light of the setting sun she saw, to her horror, what had frightened them. There on the sand lay Captain Spriggs, face down, with a dirk driven to the hilt between his shoulder blades. He was quite dead.

The footprints that must have marked the sandy soil had all been carefully erased with a branch broken from one of the peach trees. Near the body lay half of a sheet of parchment, and, in the center of that parchment, a black spot about the size of a shilling had been laboriously inscribed with a quill and black ink. The pirate mark of revenge-death.

All efforts to find the killer or killers proved futile. There were no strangers in town other than the usual polyglot assortment of sailors on leave from the many ships that lay at anchor in the harbor. There was no way to or from the island except by boat; nevertheless, it was impossible to find even one logical suspect.

As the old pirate had wished, Sea-born Woman buried him in the vault he had prepared. Sailors and local fisherman rigged a block and tackle to hoist the marble hearthstone so that the body could be lowered into the vault. Then the marble was cemented back into place to make an airtight seal. And, true to his word, Spriggs had left a will in his own handwriting, bequeathing Spriggs' Luck and all the surrounding grounds to Jerushia.

From that moment on, Jerushia lived not only in that house, but largely for that house. Always a good housekeeper, she now made a fetish of keeping Spriggs' Luck in immaculate condition. Never a speck of dust was allowed to accumulate on the fine furniture. In the spring and summer, she placed fresh flowers in the fireplace opening just alongside the marble hearthstone. Often passersby at night would see her lonely figure seated in a chair in front of the hearth, a whale-oil lamp burning brightly on a table by her side.

When the American Revolution flared into full hostilities, Ocracoke Inlet and Portsmouth Harbor became two of the focal points of combat. The deep-water channel through Ocracoke Inlet was then, as it is now, a twisting, hazardous, and ever-changing thing. Raiding British warships had to be of shallow draft to negotiate that channel, and, once inside the bar, they found American galleys, manned by patriots at the long oar sweeps, awaiting them. Resembling ancient Roman slave galleys, these oar-driven vessels were very swift and maneuverable and were usually more than a match for the slower Britishers. Thus, Portsmouth and Ocracoke harbors, as well as the Town of Portsmouth, often rang with the sound of naval gunfire, as miniature naval engagements were fought to the death in those sheltered waters.

Raiding parties of British Marines were often put ashore to

forage and to burn the countryside and kill all the livestock they could find. These invading forces were met by small groups of militia formed by the native fisherman. Usually the advantage lay with the islanders. They knew the terrain and were perfectly at home in that environment of sand and wind and roaring surf. The British had the better weapons, though, and the advantage of professional training as soldiers with the discipline of regulars. In spite of this, no actual occupation of Portsmouth Town was ever achieved by the British, although they kept considerable pressure on the thin defensive forces stationed there.

For the five or six years the fighting actually lasted on the Outer Banks, Jerushia was a tower of strength to her people. She converted Spriggs' Luck into a very efficient hospital and recruited and trained several of the local ladies as nurses. Reading avidly such medical books as she could find, she did her best to relieve, mend, and cure the casualties brought to her beloved home. The islanders had always been fond of her. Now, they began to regard her as a special saint who had been sent especially for their healing and comfort. They tipped their hats or pulled at their forelocks in gestures of respect and admiration when the tall, graceful figure, dressed always in black, walked by. They relied on her, and she never failed them as long as she lived. She was the living spirit of Portsmouth Town for many, many years, and she helped them to persevere until the Revolution was won.

Sea-born Woman died in her sleep one peaceful spring night in 1810 at the ripe old age of ninety. She was tenderly and lovingly laid to rest in the little yaupon grove to the rear of Spriggs' Luck by her friends and neighbors. There had been no illness, no suffering, no long period of disability. It is said that she just stopped living very quietly and easily.

But if the natives thought that they had seen the last of this remarkable woman when they buried her, they were mistaken. Some three years later the first recorded appearance of what is said to be her ghost took place.

During the War of 1812, when the British came so close to retaking their former American colonies, the first manifestation occurred. In 1813, the King's forces landed on Portsmouth Island and began the systematic slaughter of all the livestock they could find in order, they claimed, to procure fresh meat for their ships lying offshore. Houses were ransacked and looted, and many islanders were robbed of their few valuable possessions. It was inevitable that a fine structure like Spriggs' Luck, now boarded up and tightly shuttered, should be the object of such an attack.

An English foraging party made the mistake of breaking into the splendid old mansion one night on one of their raids. They ran into an experience none of them ever forgot. No sooner had they forced the front door and entered, torches held high for illumination, they were set upon by a whirling creature with a mane of flowing, red hair who was dressed in a long black gown.

The apparition laid about her with an oar and soon had the British in utter confusion. As if blown by some tremendous gust of wind, all the torches were extinguished in the same instant. The terrified sailors began to strike out blindly with their knives, seriously wounding several of their company. When they finally did fumble their way to the door, they beat a hasty retreat, carrying their wounded with them. Back on shipboard, they spread the word of their eerie experience, and never again was a foraging party to visit Spriggs' Luck.

Following the war, the fine old home was sold and resold many times, sometimes to people who were delighted with their purchase and sometimes to others who were terrified and wanted to get rid of it as quickly as possible. The difference was Jerushia. If she found the new owners to be lazy and inefficient housekeepers who let her home become run down and dilapidated, she would make life miserable for them with appearances and manifestations and sleepless nights until she finally drove them away. If, on the other hand, she saw that the owners took good care of Spriggs' Luck and kept it in a good state of repair, she would give them no trouble whatsoever. She had loved that house during her life, and she was not about to desert it now to unappreciative tenants.

Not only did she love and protect her former home; she also continued her interest in the islanders. Many are the tales of her help given to poor fishermen in their time of danger or of need. Often a wife in childbirth was comforted and soothed by the presence of that six-foot feminine figure with the shock of red hair. Her people did not and they do not fear her. They believe in her and respect and love her to this day for the aid and comfort she has brought a hardy, but often underprivileged, people.

For generations Spriggs' Luck stood as an inspiration and historic landmark in Portsmouth Town, but in time its luck ran out and it met the fate of all man-made structures on these Outer Banks.

It was the big hurricane, then called an equinoctial storm, of 1899 that destroyed most of what sea-born Jerushia had fought so long and so well to preserve. All during that historic storm, according to established folk memory, the natives heard wild cries of despair as the raging winds ripped and tore at the structure. The screams and the howling of the wind reached an awful crescendo at the same instant. At that second, Spriggs' Luck collapsed with a mighty roar. Board was torn from board, and the wreckage was whipped and strewn across the entire width of the island. The wind-driven tide pounded against the foundations and scattered fragments of wreckage even farther inland.

It is hard to imagine the fury of such a wind gone insane. Facing into the wind, it is impossible to breathe, and if one puts his back to the blow, it seems as though one's very lungs will be sucked from his body by that awful pressure. Tiny straws are actually blown through the trunks of small trees, so awful is the force of the moving air. Strongly built houses just disappear as if they were made of cards, and the whole appearance of a region is drastically altered in the winking of an eye. Such a storm was the 1899 disaster.

When the blow had spent its fury and the winds and seas had once again subsided, all that was left of the ancient building was the stub of a brick chimney and the massive hearthstone, now at ground level, that marked the final resting place of the old pirate. And that is all that remains today of Spriggs' Luck, now called "Brigand's Luck" by some.

Sea-born Woman did not vanish with the structure, however. Full many a sailor has stood to the wheel of his boat trying to steer a safe course through fog or driving rain to enter Ocracoke Inlet and has suddenly become aware of a tall, willowy figure standing by his side, mahogany hair floating free in the wind and long arm and forefinger pointing the way to safe passage. Still the tall, graceful figure can be seen on rare occasions as she moves about that marble slab. Sometimes, they say, if you listen very carefully and remain very still, you can hear the faint sound of gay laughter and the music of long, long ago.

New Berne's Bleeding Arch

from *Blackbeard's Cup and Stories of the Outer Banks*

The city of New Berne (now shortened to New Bern) is one of the most beautiful and historic cities in the South. Its citizens, as are the citizens of Edenton, Bath, and other coastal settlements, are blessed with a God-given sense of history. The magnificent restoration of Governor Tryon's colonial palace is a perfect example of the reverence these people feel for their Swiss-American heritage.

Named after the city of Berne in Switzerland, New Berne was settled by Baron DeGraffenreid and the Palatines, artisans from Switzerland and Germany, in the late 1600s under the aegis of England. From that early date until today, it has played a prominent part in the history of North Carolina, some of which is known and some of which, unfortunately, can only be surmised. Situated at the junction of the Neuse and Trent Rivers, New Berne was very accessible to the sailing ships of the day. It was, indeed, a deep water outpost in the new continent. So ancient is a part of the town that the framework of the original Anglican Church is still preserved there. In this early house of worship the dead were buried beneath the floor of the nave of the church to keep the Indians from knowing of any weakening of the town's strength.

On Queen Street, also in the heart of the "old town" of New Berne, one can still find a very old cemetery called Cedar Grove Cemetery. Commanding a beautiful view of the broad sweep of the Neuse River, this truly ante-many-bellum burying ground is the location of many fascinating legends and stories. Some of these appear to have real elements of truth, while others are apparently pure folk legend and may have sprung from some historical event.

The cemetery was conveyed in the year 1800 to Christ Church. The church itself was already an ancient landmark at the time, although it was in beautiful condition (it still is and is used daily by its Episcopal congregation down to this good hour). Christ Church "opened" the cemetery in that same year and it has been in use, with many enlargements, to the present.

The old part of Cedar Grove Cemetery is enclosed by an equally ancient stone wall, and entrance is gained through a very imposing stone arch. The wall and the arch were constructed by local masons with large blocks of what the natives call "shell stone." This material, which is quarried locally, far from the distant mountains, is composed of millions of ossified sea shells and the fossilized skeletons of other large and small sea creatures. These little beings sank to the bottom of the Atlantic Ocean, which at that time covered New Berne. Over millions of years, they gradually hardened into a sort of coral-like stone in which you can clearly see the outlines of the sea shells. This material is very hard, like stone, but it can be cut fairly easily into large blocks. The masons of that day used these blocks well in constructing with great skill and loving care both the wall and the imposing archway of the entrance.

The cemetery itself is unusual and historic, but it is also marked by a fascinating phenomenon. Since the memory of man runneth not to the contrary, the archway has been used as the entrance for funeral processions into the burial ground. Its generous width provides plenty of room for the casket and the pallbearers on either side. From that day to this, such processions are greeted by the dripping of what appears to be blood upon the mourners passing beneath the arch. Not a stream, mind you, but a slow and temporary drip, drip, drip and then a halt. This substance is red, it is slightly sticky, there is no apparent source, and it always drops on funerals in a sequence of three drops, then a pause, then three more drops, then another pause, and so on.

One of the legends concerning this arch, held with conviction by some of the older residents, states that if one or more of the drops fall upon the head of one of the pallbearers, that person will be the next out of that group to die and be carried through that same arch. They even quote some rather startling statistics to prove their point, giving names and dates!

There are other stories relating to the arch and at least one of them is based on the early history of this country. It concerns a duel that should never have happened and a tragedy that resulted in a great loss to North Carolina and the nation.

New Berne produced many stalwart sons who played important parts in the early history of the region. The Baron DeGraffenreid, although Swiss by birth, was certainly a New Bernian, as was John Lawson, the Surveyor General of the Crown Colony, and Governor Eden, along with many, many others. One of the more well-known was a man named Richard Dobbs Spaight. He was very active in the formation not only of Carolina but also of the nation. He was one of the first governors of the state of North Carolina, and he devoted his entire life to serving his region, his state, and his fledgling nation. He practiced law in New Berne when he was not holding some public office. He was widely known and loved by almost everyone.

Politics being what they are (and ever have been), Governor Spaight in 1802 became embroiled in a spirited difference of political philosophy with a man named John Stanly, another New Bernian of some importance. He was a lawyer of considerable ability and was noted, most of all, for his fortes of invective and sarcasm. In his later years he was elected to the State Legislature, where he served with distinction. He served as Speaker of the House and ruled that chamber with a rod of iron.

The story is told that, when General Lafayette visited the new United States in 1825, Stanly introduced a bill to appropriate considerable money with which to give the general an appropriate North Carolina welcome. He was bitterly opposed on this bill by a number of conservative members, and it was thought that the vote would be a close one. When the vote was called for, Stanly arose from his Speaker's seat, called another member to preside in his stead, and then, glaring down at his opponents, roared: "Mr. Speaker, I, too, desire to put every member on record so that if any one votes against this bill he may be gibbeted high up on the pillory of infamy." Strong language, even for those days, and words that could have easily led to a challenge to a duel. It is recorded that every man, somewhat awed, voted "Aye" and the bill passed unanimously. Such was the ability and the temperament of Governor Spaight's adversary.

The debate in New Berne between John Stanly and Governor

Spaight grew acrimonious and, in the fashion of the day, it was proposed that the difference be settled by a duel to the death. Thus, a challenge was issued and accepted and arrangements were made for the "field of honor," in which marksmanship and luck would be called upon to decide who was right and who was wrong.

It was to be pistols at an agreed distance and firing upon signal. Spaight was a man of peace and was unused to using a firearm, but his honor demanded that he abide by the rules and seek to kill or be killed by his fellow lawyer. It seems incredible today that men of the intelligence of those involved should engage in such illogical behavior, but dueling according to a strict *code duello* was the order of the day and the two men were locked into the situation.

Thus it was that the "field of honor" was chosen, set up, and prepared by the "seconds" of each man. The location of the encounter was chosen—a very pleasant alley paved with handmade brick and situated just a few hundred yards from Cedar Grove Cemetery.

There, very early on the morning of September 5, both Stanly and Spaight showed up dressed in their very best clothing. Each was accompanied by a second. There were a few other witnesses there, too, some of them sensation seekers but most of them deeply concerned citizens. These very earnest men pleaded with the principals to find some other way to settle their differences. Spaight might have agreed to this if an honorable way could have been found, but it is said that Stanly seemed thirsty for blood and that he cut short this discussion of alternatives.

The seconds then brought forward a brace, or pair of pistols, in a mahogany, velvet-lined case. The weapons looked and probably were identical, and each was loaded with the same amount of powder and the same size shot. The principals were then each shown the exact spot on which to stand so that the rising sun would be in neither man's eyes and were told to await the signal. Spaight and Stanly each took his weapon, glanced at it, and then walked slowly and deliberately to his assigned station. The early morning sun was beginning to light the tops of the trees and a few birds began to greet the dawn of a beautiful, early fall day with song. Down on the field of honor there was a deathly silence.

Off to one side of the intended line of fire the seconds and the spectators waited as the elder of the seconds held aloft his white, silk handkerchief.

"Gentlemen," he said, "I shall now count to three. At the count of three, I shall release this handkerchief and you may fire at will. You do not have to wait until the handkerchief touches the ground but may fire at the count of three. And now, please take aim. One, two . . ."

At the count of three, as the handkerchief fluttered downward, the two pistols roared as one. Strangely, both shots missed their mark and the duelists stood unharmed.

The pistols were reloaded and, once again, the two statesmen fired at each other. Once again they both missed! The spectators had grown in number as the firing continued, and now they redoubled their efforts to effect a compromise but things had apparently gone too far. Shots had been fired and under the *code duello* the whole thing could have been called off then with no shame to anyone, but this was not to be. This time, the two principals were placed ten steps apart facing away from each other. They were handed reloaded pistols and told to wheel and fire at the given word. It is thought that the seconds were trying to increase the likelihood of another miss and perhaps reduce the duel to an absurdity but, when the word was given, an entirely different result occurred. Whether intentionally or not, Governor Spaight's bullet missed Stanly and imbedded itself in a brick wall. Stanly's bullet sped straight and true and struck Spaight in the chest, inflicting a mortal wound from which he died in a very short time.

Thus, North Carolina was deprived of one of its brightest and most patriotic sons in the very prime of his life and at a time when his leadership was critically needed. Stanly, still bloodthirsty, soon thereafter tried to pick a quarrel with Spaight's son with the avowed intention, it is said, of challenging the boy to a duel and thus ridding himself once and for all of not one but two of his opponents.

After the duel, it was first thought that Governor Spaight would be buried in Cedar Grove Cemetery and it is said that a grave was opened there to receive his body. His family, however, decided that he should be buried on land owned by the family and located just west of the town of New Berne. It is there that his last resting place is preserved to this day.

Public indignation blazed against Stanly and there was talk of seeing to it that he was justly punished one way or another. He had abided by the *code duello* to the letter, however, and other than being shunned by many of his former friends, he was never brought to account for Spaight's death.

There are those in New Berne who say that the majestic arch at Cedar Grove has not forgotten his death. They say that the drops of blood continue to call, even at this late day, for vengeance. Drip, drip, drip—avenge Spaight's blood, drip, drip, drip—avenge Spaight's blood. And those drops surely do look like blood and feel like blood to the touch.

Some explain them by surmising that the masons who constructed the stonework used notched iron spikes between the topmost stones of the arch—spikes which today are invisible to the naked eye because of the way they were embedded between the stones. They say that these iron spikes have continued to rust away over the years and that the moisture of rains, soaked up by the semiporous stone, supply the liquid that causes the arch to drip, drip, drip.

True it is that the arch does not bleed solely on the occasion of funerals—it bleeds at other times and at no predictable intervals. But it is also true that when it does bleed, it bleeds in groups of three consecutive drops, never more, never less, just as the seconds' count of "One, two, three" was in cadence at the duel and just as the slogan, "Avenge Spaight's blood," is in the same cadence.

Whether or not you believe any of the legends associated with the ancient arch, it would seem to be the sensible thing to try to avoid being struck by the drops. The very least that can happen is that you may incur an expensive dry cleaning or laundry bill.

What do you think?

The Flaming Ship of Ocracoke

from *The Flaming Ship of Ocracoke & Other Tales of the Outer Banks*

Some most unusual things continue to happen just off the northern shore of Ocracoke Inlet. Of course, this region is known the world over as a part of the Graveyard of the Atlantic, and many are the tales of shipwrecks and sailors lost at sea and of treasures lying buried beneath the shifting sands of the Diamond Shoals. Most of these legends have no recurring manifestations; but the Ocracoke Happening, they say, repeats itself year after year, always under the same conditions and always at the same spot. Many people have seen it time after time, and always on the night when the new moon makes its first appearance in September. Thus, the dates may differ from year to year, but that sliver of new moon is always part of the scene.

In the region itself, the most widely accepted explanation is a combination of history and folk memory which has been told and retold by the older fisherman to their sons and grandsons. Many of these old-timers may not be able to name the current Secretary of the Interior, but they can tell you, with amazing accuracy, of the time when Anne was Queen of England and many efforts were being made to colonize the Carolinas. This was a time when the continent of Europe was in a ferment. The tiny German Palatinate had been overrun, time and again, by the vicious wars between Catholic and Protestant armies. The people were weary with so-called religious wars, and they longed for peace.

In the beautiful Rhine River Valley in 1689, the retreating armies of Louis XIV had brutally scourged and laid waste the entire countryside, leaving everything destroyed and most of the people destitute. Some ten thousand Palatines, as they were called, flooded into England for refuge, and the authorities did not know what to do with them. No beggars, these, but honest and skilled craftsmen, miners, and artisans of the first order. Such an influx of jobless thousands threw the British economy completely out of kilter.

The British people, though sympathetic at first, soon began to complain, so the English Queen listened with favor when the Swiss Baron Christophe DeGraffenried, eager to mend his own personal fortunes and to solve the problems of many of the Palatines at the same time, proposed taking several hundred of these poor people to the Province of Carolina in the New World across the sea. England desperately needed colonists, and the Palatines just as desperately needed new homes, so Queen Anne told DeGraffenried to go ahead with his plan.

The mass migration, organized and directed by the good baron, was beset by trials and tribulations, but it finally resulted in the settlement of a large portion of land in what is now eastern North Carolina. The settelement was known, at first, by the Indian name Chattoka. Today it is identified as the beautiful city of New Bern (formerly New Berne). Many people know of these fine Swiss and German folk who have meant so much to the history of North Carolina and of their leader, Baron DeGraffenried, the Landgrave of Carolina.

Most people, though, do not know about a later shipload of Palatines whose financial status was much better but whose destiny was not to be so bright. While homeless, they were still possessed of a large amount of gold and silver plate, gold candlesticks, and many valuable coins and jewels, which they had managed to conceal from invading armies. Whereas the earlier Palatines had come to America by means of financing furnished by the British government, these later emigrants paid for their own passage by subscription among themselves. They, too, were looking for a new and better home in Carolina. They had heard good reports of the colony from their friends who had come over with DeGraffenried and were eager to make their own beginnings in that new land.

The passage from England was uneventful, as day followed sunny day, and the ship made good time. The hopes of these thrifty Palatines were high as they looked forward to soon joining their countrymen in New Berne. Each of them had been very careful to conceal his precious possessions in the sea bags and chests allowed in the sleeping quarters below decks. So far as could be seen, they were just as poor as their friends who had come before them.

At that time, Ocracoke Inlet was the principal point of entry for ships with passengers or cargoes bound for the interior of North Carolina. Ocean-going vessels could negotiate the inlet and sail over the shallow sounds to the inland cities, or they could, and usually did, anchor just inside or outside the inlet and transfer the passengers or cargoes to smaller boats which were bound for New Berne, Bath, or Edenton. Travelers were usually given a few hours in which to stretch their legs and walk about in Portsmouth Town before beginning the final lap of their journey.

Thus it was with the ship carrying these later Palatines. They arrived offshore before dawn and anchored in the calm waters just to the seaward from Ocracoke Inlet. The passengers were in a fever of excitement. Lights could be seen from the houses on the nearby shore, and the smell of woodsmoke from the early morning cooking fires in Pilot Town (now called Ocracoke Village) carried across the water to the pilgrims. The children were the most enthusiastic of all as they ran back and forth on the deck, laughing and playing. The perilous sea voyage was over, and they were now only a short distance from their new homes.

Among the adults, there was more sober talk of Indians and whether or not they would continue to be friendly, of gold mines, and of the prospect of living without the constant threat of war. It was a time of new beginnings. They believed that they had, at last, found a fresh page on which to write their own personal histories.

By the time it was fully daylight, all the Palatines were dressed in their best clothes and were assembled on the deck of the ship. They were eager to set foot on land and to see the sights of Portsmouth Town. Not wanting to risk the theft of valuables, they made the mistake of bringing these belongings up on deck with them. There they stood, their eyes full of hope and anticipation and their hands full of more treasure than the ship's captain had ever seen in any one place in his entire lifetime.

Unknown to his passengers, the Captain had, at one time, been a pirate, but he had taken the "King's Pardon," promising to lead a law-abiding life. At the sight of the Palatines' treasure, however, his new moral code promptly went by the board. Calling a hurried meeting with his crew, the skipper found them all of a like mind to his. This was too easy a chance to be missed.

So the plot was laid. The Captain told his passengers that there had been some delay in arranging their transportation to New Berne, but he promised to take care of that by the next morning. He advised them to return to their quarters below decks and to get some rest against the rigors of the next stage of their travels, as they would not be able to go ashore until the next day. This the Palatines did, taking their belongings with them, not even questioning the fact that the Captain had waved away several small boats and lighters which had come out to get the business of taking passengers and their belongings ashore.

The night that followed was the first night of the new moon in that September of long ago. The sun had set some hours before, and the new moon was low in the sky when the crew, led by the Captain and both mates, slipped up behind the few passengers taking the air on deck and silently strangled them with short lengths of line. Then, silently and swiftly, they crept below, knives in hand, and cut the throats of every remaining passenger, children as well as adults. Not one was spared.

These brutal murders accomplished, the crew then brought lights into the hold and methodically ripped open all the sea bags and chests belonging to the murdered people, stealing all the gold, silver, jewels, and coins they had so much coveted on the deck of the ship that morning. Pirate-like, they divided their loot on the deck of the ship. Then, lowering the ship's longboat into the sea, they prepared to go ashore. Just before they left the ship, they spread the vessel's mainsail and jib and slipped the anchor chain so that the craft could run before the gentle southwest wind. As a final touch, the captain set fire to the large pile of rifled sea bags and chests which had been heaped near the mainmast. This was to make more credible the tale of disaster they intended to tell when they reached the shore.

About halfway to shore, the men rested their oars and looked back at the ship. The Captain turned his head, too, and saw that the fire had spread more rapidly than he had anticipated. Apparently the lines holding the furled topsails and topgallantsails to the yard had burned in two. Now, all the sails seemed to be set, and the ship was driving at full speed, not in a northeasterly direction but almost due west, right toward the crowded longboat.

The sails seemed to be solid sheets of flame, and from the hold of the burning ship came long, loud, pitiful wails, filling the dark sea with the mournful sounds of souls in torment. The inferno ship bore down upon the frantically fleeing longboat until, with a crash of splintering timbers, it rolled the doomed little craft over and over under its keel, spilling the murderer-robbers into the sea. Most of them drowned outright. Some, however, were able to cling to pieces of wreckage from the longboat until they were washed ashore many hours later. Amazingly, the burning death ship then came about and, with no living soul at her lashed helm, set a steady course toward the northeast again, her sails still aflame and the mournful wails still emanating from the hold.

To this day, they say, that flaming ship reappears on the first night of the new moon in September. Her sails are always sheets of flame and her rigging glows red-hot in the near darkness. Always there is the accompanying eerie wailing, as she sails swiftly and purposefully toward the northeast. Three times she runs her ghostly course on each occasion. She always seems to sail from the water just offshore to a point where she can barely be seen as a small glow on the distant horizon. They say she will sail out of sight; and then, twice again, she will suddenly reappear just offshore and sail toward the northeast. Those who have seen her say you can always smell the odor of burning canvas and hemp, and she always moves northeastward, regardless of the direction and velocity of the wind.

So far is known, not one single piece of the treasure belonging to the doomed Palatines has ever been washed up on the beach. So far as can be told, the flaming ship will continue to sail her fiery course each year while those betrayed pilgrims continue to look for peace and happiness in that new home to which they came so near.

Currituck Jack

from *Outer Banks Mysteries & Seaside Stories*

The war of the American Revolution dragged on into the late seventeen hundreds. The British redcoats still occupied New York, and the British fleet still maintained a fairly effective naval blockade to the south, including the coast of North Carolina. Coastwise trade of the colonies was severely curtailed, and our fledgling navy was badly in need of the supplies and naval stores that eastern Carolina had in such abundance.

Up in Currituck County, near what is now known as Currituck Courthouse, there lived a middle-aged man, Caleb White, a devout Quaker and an American patriot, who was also a skilled shipbuilder by profession. He not only built beautiful and seaworthy vessels, but he sailed them as well, carrying vital cargoes up and down the coast in the face of the blockade. This was his contribution to the American war effort. Admittedly it was profitable, but it was also exciting, and it allowed him to satisfy the demands of his patriotism without violating his religious beliefs.

The business was not without its risks. In 1778 White had lost one of his finest ships when it was captured and confiscated by the British blockade, and that was painful both to his pocketbook and to his seaman's pride. He always believed, did Caleb, that if he had been in command of that ship, she would never have been captured. But all that was in the past.

In 1779 Caleb White joined in a partnership with his cousin, Henry White, and they set out to build another blockade runner that would be capable of slipping through the British stranglehold, both because of her speed and because her low profile would make her very difficult to see. But they also had the pressing duty of designing and building the perfect shipping vessel, one that would be sufficiently broad of beam to accommodate a large cargo.

In the fall of 1779 she was completed and ready for the sea, and she was quite a thing of beauty to behold. Christened the *Polly*, she was a two-masted, schooner-type ship built with loving care out of juniper and cypress and heart-pine wood. She was broad of beam, but with relatively little freeboard, so that she would lie low in the water. Her jib boom extended a little farther than was usual in ships of her size, which gave room for the extra jib she would carry. This extra sail was calculated to give her greater speed and maneuverability and to counteract her broadness of beam.

Below deck, just abaft the mainmast, there was a comfortable cabin complete with bunks and a little cookstove. Two large hatches on the deck gave access to the cargo holds below, and over these were stout hatch covers whose outer surfaces were tarred canvas. Her hull, masts, and spars were painted black, and her sails were dyed dark brown. She would be hard to catch and even hard to see in poor light.

The two partners, Captain Caleb and cousin Henry White,

watched with pride as she slid down into the waters of the North Landing River just a short distance upstream from where that river empties into the waters of Currituck Sound. Caleb was determined to command the *Polly* himself and not risk her fate with someone less experienced at her wheel. To lose this ship to the British would just about bankrupt him. Henry White, for his part, was in complete agreement with the plan. He had a sizable investment in the *Polly*, as well as an equally strong desire to help the struggling colonists win their war of independence. Henry was too old to go seafaring, but he was perfectly content to trust his investment to the skilled hands and eyes of Captain Caleb.

Now, cousin Henry White was a man of considerable wealth by the standards of that day. Not only did he own several large farms, but he also had inherited from an uncle, several years before our story, a young African slave boy named Jack. This lad was said to have come from the Watusi tribe and to have been kidnapped by a Yankee trader and sold to Henry's uncle in the slave market in Charleston. The purchaser took an almost immediate liking to the boy, and he raised him more like a son than a servant. When Henry inherited Jack at the uncle's death, he continued the kind and considerate treatment Jack was used to, and the young fellow grew into one of the finest physical specimens ever seen around Currituck County.

He was nearly seven feet tall, as were his ancestors, but the physical development he achieved was outstanding. He weighed nearly three hundred pounds, but there was practically no fat on him. He was broad of shoulder, narrow of waist, and as quick as a cat on his feet. He could run faster and lift greater weights than any man around. He soon developed into a local celebrity.

Along with his magnificent physique, Jack had developed a personality and a character that were equally fine. He had flourished and prospered under the kind treatment he had received, and his quick mind had eagerly absorbed all the education his owners were able to furnish him. With this he combined a gentle nature and a kind and loving regard for all around him. He was fiercely devoted to his new country and was just as proud of her efforts for freedom as any man was. Jack was a sincere patriot.

You see, the young man had an even deeper interest in freedom than did most men. He was, after all, a slave himself. Though his two owners had always been generous and fair with him, he wanted very much to be free. He longed to be free to remain in this blessed land and to set up his own home. He wanted to marry his own wife and raise his own family and make his own way in the world.

Understanding this universal longing to be free, Jack's original owner had set up for him on the books of his business what was called a "manumittal account." Henry White had continued this account after he inherited the boy.

The practice, which was not at all unusual in the area at the time, consisted of an arrangement whereby a slave could actually "buy" himself back. Any time a slave rendered an unusually meritorious service or had to work unusually long or demanding hours, he was given credit on his manumittal account. If he preferred, he could have Christmas gifts and birthday presents and other occasional gratuities credited as a money credit on the account rather than receive them in cash or in kind.

In time this could, and often did, mount up to a sum that was equal to the purchase price formerly paid for the slave with, possibly, a small amount of interest added. When this occurred, there was a great ceremony of manumission, or freeing, of the person involved. Official records were entered at the courthouse or nearest seat of government. They proclaimed and gave public notice that the manumitted individual was henceforward and for all time a free and independent person with the right to own property (including slaves of his own), to make contracts, and in all other ways to conduct himself as any other free man.

Although still in his twenties, Jack had accumulated quite a respectable sum in his manumittal account, and the community where he lived took it for granted that he would eventually earn his freedom and that the respected black would soon take his place in the fabric of coastal life as a free man.

Henry White trusted the young slave so completely that he assigned him to sail with Captain Caleb White when the *Polly* undertook her maiden voyage. Jack knew navigation as well as anyone his age, and he was perfectly at home on shipboard.

Small as she was, the *Polly* would need three persons to sail her efficiently. The third crew member was eventually found in the person of one Samuel Jasper, who was also an accomplished waterman and was about Jack's age. Although not nearly a physical match for the large slave, Sam was strong and alert, and he was a man of temperate habits and judgment. He was also Captain Caleb's brother-in-law and a much beloved member of the family.

A fine crew for any vessel: Captain Caleb, the able-bodied brother-in-law, and the huge and powerful Jack. All hands were satisfied that the *Polly* was not only well found but well manned also. At last they were ready to tweak the nose of the British lion.

And thus it was that the schooner *Polly*, loaded with naval stores of pitch and tar and turpentine, with barrels of corn, and even with a few bales of dried yaupon bushes to furnish tea for the ladies of the blockaded cities, was ready to undertake her first attempt to help break the enemy blockade.

February 14, 1780, the day of departure, dawned cold and

overcast. There was a definite threat of snow, and a gentle breeze held steady from the west. Captain Caleb, Jack, and Sam Jasper were all aboard early, as they wanted to catch the favorable tide for their journey down the sound to the open sea. The families and a few friends were on hand to wish them godspeed and a safe voyage. There were firm handshakes all around and a few bearlike embraces, and the three mariners went aboard the *Polly*, which was moored at "the Launch," where Tull Bay empties with a fair flow of water into the North Landing River.

A single jib was raised to pull the *Polly*'s head out into the current caused by the ebbing tide, and she was on her way. As she cleared the Launch with Captain Caleb at the wheel, Jack and Sam raised the mainsail, which filled beautifully with the westerly breeze. Responsive to her helm, the *Polly* headed proudly out across the river in the general direction of Knott's Island, following the well-known channel to Currituck Sound.

A few flakes of snow began falling as they ran their casting down and raised Halfway Point on their port beam. The wind increased, as did the snow, as they turned now more southerly and sailed out onto the broad expanse of Currituck Sound. They had decided to sail out into the Atlantic through Caffey's Inlet, near where the present community of Corolla is located. Oregon Inlet was not in existence at that time, and Hatteras and Ocracoke Inlets were too well patrolled by the British for them to risk running the blockade at either of those two inlets. The wiser choice and the closer route was through Caffey's Inlet, unmarked though it was.

None of the crew felt any misgivings about the weather. They knew this water as they knew the backs of their own hands, and once out onto the Atlantic, the plan was to sail at least forty or fifty miles offshore to avoid the blockade before turning north to run parallel with the coastline. This last heading would be by compass bearing and by dead reckoning, and no one was better at that type of sailing than was Captain Caleb White.

Down the sound they sailed in high spirits, joining now and then in singing sea chanties, with Sam doing an intricate sailor's jig for the entertainment of the others. It was not yet time to begin their regular routine of one man at the wheel, one man to tend the sails, and one man asleep belowdecks.

The favorable breeze grew fitful and the snow increased as they neared Caffey's Inlet. What breeze there was continued to hold fair, however, and they glided through the difficult channels of the inlet under a full set of sails just as darkness fell. This met Captain Caleb's plan exactly. With this timing, one of the most dangerous parts of the trip would be made under the cover of darkness. So far, so good.

On they sped into the gathering darkness. The bow of the *Polly* began to rise and fall as she met the long, even ground swell of the North Atlantic, the pathway to beleaguered Boston but also largely a British sea. Britannia still ruled the waves, by and large, and her capable seamen were determined to choke the life out of the American uprising.

As she began to make her first long easterly run to get sea room, the *Polly* began to encounter patches of fog. The full moon shed only a ghostly light over the ocean as it settled lower and lower, the fog all but blotting out its beauty. It was reduced to an indistinct, silvery blob in the sky, useful for determining the approximate directions but furnishing no illumination to speak of.

Already running without lights to avoid detection, the *Polly* was almost completely concealed. Thus she gained not only an added measure of protection, but she incurred added danger as well. Simply because she could not be seen, she ran the greater risk of being run down by any passing ship that happened to be on a collision course with her route eastward.

All that night she ran before the faint westerly wind with Jack at the wheel, steering entirely by the ship's compass. Captain Caleb was sound asleep in the little cabin. As there was little need to change the set of the sails during the entire night, Sam Jasper employed himself in restacking the firewood piled on deck. From time to time he would pause in this chore and talk with the helmsman. Forward progress was extremely slow, and the night was bone-chilling cold.

The next day, February 15, began with a heavily overcast sky and a wind that shifted to the northeast during midmorning and increased steadily. The fog bank drifted away to the south, where it hung like a great gray wall under the leaden sky. All that day the *Polly* ran into the wind and drifted under shortened sail as the wind grew stronger and stronger by the hour. As though to add to their difficulties, a freezing rain began to fall, and the little ship labored as she met the increasing waves almost head on. At sunset it was determined not to sail through the night, since they were already well out to sea. Instead, it was decided to heave the *Polly* to and ride out the night while all the three-man crew tried to get a good night's sleep in the warmth of the little cabin.

A drogue, or sea anchor, was put out to hold the *Polly*'s bow into the waves and to make her ride more comfortably and safely. This consisted of several oars and pieces of firewood lashed together into a sort of raft that floated in the water and was secured by a line to the bow of the schooner. Being lower in the water and not so much affected by the wind as the ship was, the drogue drifted more slowly than the boat and thus held the line taut. The line, in turn, tended to hold the bow of the ship pointed directly into the waves. Of course, the ship then drifted southwestward, but at a very slow speed, and Captain

Caleb was sure that he had plenty of sea room. Every two or three hours, one of the crew would come up on deck to check the way the *Polly* was riding and to see that all was well.

On that very same night, and unknown to anyone aboard the *Polly,* the British man-of-war *Fame* was also hove to for the night and was also riding at a sea anchor and drifting slowly southwestward. She was part of the blockade fleet, but she had gotten badly off course during the winter storm, and her captain was afraid she might be too near Cape Hatteras for safety. He prudently decided to wait until daylight before continuing his southerly course for Charleston.

H.M.S. *Fame* was a splendid fighting ship of some fifteen cannon and a complement of British marines in addition to her own smartly trained crew. She carried a veritable cloud of sail under fair weather conditions, and she was considered to be a most able vessel for blockade duty. Nobody aboard the *Fame* knew then that just a few miles to the leeward, the American schooner lay dead in the water with only bare rigging exposed to the gale.

Of course, riding higher in the water and with a great deal more rigging and masts and spars exposed to that gale, the *Fame* was drifting faster than the *Polly*, and so the gap between the two was gradually closing as the night wore on.

"Sail, ho," cried Jack from the masthead to which he had climbed to free a snarled pulley, and "Sail, ho," sang out the watch from the mizzentop of the man-of-war.

Both ships exploded into frantic activity.

The two ships had sighted each other at the same instant, and at the time of the sighting no more than three miles of open water separated the two crafts.

It was obvious to Captain Caleb when he had focused his telescope on the warship that she was a British blockader, and it was equally obvious to Captain Maher of the *Fame* that he was looking at a fat prize of a blockade runner. Both the hunter and the hunted knew what they must do.

Neither captain bothered to retrieve his sea drogue but cut it loose in his haste to pile on sail. Both wanted to get under way with as much headway as possible just as soon as possible. The *Polly* was downwind from the *Fame*, so her best bet was to turn "on her heel" and run for all she was worth. Captain Maher knew instantly that his best course was to give pursuit until he could bring his intended prize within range of his bow gun.

In a gale such as was developing, the *Fame* had all the advantage. She carried more sail and higher sail than did the *Polly*, and Captain Maher felt confident that if he did not swamp his boat under the added sail, he could overtake the fleeing schooner. True, a stern chase is always a long chase, but he felt he could pull the trick off with prudent increases in sail area and patience in slowly overhauling his prey.

Captain Caleb, on the contrary, felt that if he could keep his lead for several hours, he might be able to duck into that fog bank he had left the day before, if it were still there. Then, he thought, he could take evasive action and elude the Britisher.

Most stern chases are indeed long chases, and this one proved to be no exception. The *Fame*, while she gained steadily on the *Polly*, did not overtake her with the speed Captain Maher wished, and the little schooner managed to find the fog bank and slip into it before the man-of-war's cannon could be brought to bear.

Captain Caleb White had won the first round.

Now, trying to outguess the other captain, Caleb spun the wheel and headed the *Polly* on a southeasterly course, thinking that the Britisher would assume that the *Polly* would run under cover of the fog for the protection of the shore and would chase after her in that direction.

It would have been better for the three shipmates if she had indeed run for the shore.

After sailing for several hours at top speed in that southeasterly direction, the *Polly* burst from the fog bank and into clear weather, only to find that the *Fame* had duplicated her maneuver. The British ship had, unknowingly, run a course parallel with that of the *Polly* until she had approached within a few hundred yards off the *Polly*'s port beam. And there the man-of-war was, boiling along "with a bone in her teeth" and still upwind from the *Polly*.

The jig was up. At least it was up as far as the race between the two vessels was concerned. A well-aimed shot from the British ship whistled across the *Polly*'s bow, and another came even closer as it whined beyond the schooner and splashed into the sea. Thus, obviously within cannon range and having nothing to fight back with, the only course for the Americans was to heave to and await the command of their captors. The *Polly* was a prize of war, and her three-man crew was captive.

A boarding party from the warship was not long in coming. The *Fame*'s jolly boat came dancing over the waves, rounded the stern of the little schooner, and then threw grappling hooks over the starboard rails. Up and over the rails and onto the heaving deck of the *Polly* came the crew of the jolly boat, followed by Captain Maher himself.

You see, both skippers had been correct in their strategy. Captain Caleb was correct in guessing that Captain Maher would assume that the *Polly* would make a run for shore. That's exactly what the Britisher did think the probabilities were. What the Carolina skipper did not know was that Maher did not know exactly where he was. A clumsy midshipman had dropped the captain's sextant five days earlier, and as a result, all Maher could be sure of was that he was somewhere off the Virginia Capes. He did know that the dangerous Platt Shoals lay somewhere to his south, and beyond that lay Wimble Shoals, and then, most dreaded of all, Diamond Shoals. It was no flight of fancy which had named that area the "Graveyard of the Atlantic."

The British skipper had no intention of taking the risk of running the *Fame* aground and having her break up around him. He was well aware that he would have less chance of catching the *Polly* if he headed the *Fame* to the southeast, but he also knew he would be running less chance of losing his ship to the stormy shoal water. He wanted sea room for his vessel first of all. Second, he wanted to capture the *Polly*.

As the fates decreed it, he got both his wishes. There the *Polly* lay on the surface of the stormy sea, scarcely two days and less than a hundred miles into her maiden voyage, and she was a captive, a prize of war.

After inspecting the captured ship as best he could in the squally weather, Captain Maher detailed five of his men to stay aboard the *Polly* as a prize crew and sail her to New York, which was still in the hands of the British forces. Her naval stores could be put to good use in maintaining the warships based there, and her corn would help nourish the occupying troops ashore.

Captain White, Currituck Jack, and Sam Jasper were placed in irons brought over from the British ship and were then lashed to the mainmast on deck, where they could be kept in plain sight of the helmsman. The five limeys intended to sail the *Polly* to New York with no help from her former crew. She was now a British ship.

With a dip of her colors in salute, the *Fame*, with Captain Maher back on board and now in a very good mood, came back before the wind and sailed off in a southerly direction for the Charleston blockade.

As if in sympathy with the spirits of the American shipmates, both the barometer and the thermometer began to drop steadily.

A freezing rain began to fall. The wind, already strong and out of the northeast, gradually increased until it was blowing a full gale and developed into a typical north Atlantic storm. Everyone aboard the *Polly* was miserable and cold.

Later that afternoon the sailor on watch on deck discovered some unusual activity among the prisoners on the foredeck. Upon investigation it was found that Caleb and Sam had almost succeeded in working loose the ropes binding the giant slave. Another five minutes of such effort and he would have been free to move about the pitching decks of the *Polly*. Jack was quickly secured and tied, this time spread-eagle on his back and lying face-up into the driving rain. For further security and to keep that escape attempt from happening again, the other two Americans were herded down into the forehold of the ship, where they were securely tied.

Belowdecks it was cold but dry, and the two white men could feel every pitch and swoop of the laboring vessel magnified several times. Luckily, neither Captain Caleb White nor Sam Jasper was subject to seasickness. Cold ship's biscuits from the *Fame* and cold water were given to them twice a day, and they were closely watched while they ate the simple fare.

If it was bad in the hold it was pure, freezing hell on that foredeck. With no protection at all from the elements, Jack lay on his back, the freezing rain beating down on his prostrate figure. Every once in a while a breaking sea would sluice along the deck, bringing even more misery. It would have killed an ordinary human being.

All afternoon long and all that interminable night, the giant black man suffered through torture few men have had to endure. From time to time a thin coating of ice would form on the outer garments of the huge prisoner as the freezing rain continued to fall in a steady downpour.

The *Polly* was making no progress at all. The weather was just too rough, so the British seamen were content to let her ride, as before, at a sea anchor and with no sails set. The little vessel continued to lie there on the surface of the troubled sea, just waiting out the storm until conditions were more favorable.

The next morning, when Jack was brought his breakfast of cold bread and water, his captor broached the subject of forsaking his American colleagues and joining the British cause. After all, the British seaman argued, Jack had known nothing but slavery at the hands of Americans, and he was in his own present miserable condition because he had thrown his lot in with the colonists. It was an attention-getting argument.

All that morning the prize crew took turns talking with Jack, always in the same vein. "Come over to us," they pleaded, "and we can promise you a warm cabin and good food for now and your own freedom when we reach New York." "The American cause is doomed," they argued. "At most, all you can expect from them is continued slavery. With us, a man of your strength and skills could join the Royal Navy and make a wonderful career for himself. We can get the Royal Governor of New York to make you a free man as soon as we reach that city." And so on and so on, all through that forenoon, as Jack's misery grew and the chill invaded his very bones.

Jack would have been less than human if he had not considered their arguments. After all, he was a slave. Freedom, his own personal freedom, was something he had longed for all his life. If only he could believe these sailors, believe that freedom was now his for the asking. Could he turn traitor to his friends and his adopted country?

What Jack could not and did not know was that this was a standard British trick used literally hundreds of times in usually successful efforts to persuade slaves to run away to the British.

Once their loyalty was gained, the men were not freed at all. When their usefulness to the British cause had been served, they were sold back into slavery, usually under much more severe conditions than the ones they had left. The invaders treated them as so much captured contraband.

Jack began to think back upon his own life as a slave. He remembered how he had hunted and fished with these shipmates of his and others in Currituck. He recalled how he had been treated more like a brother than a slave or even a servant. He thought of how he had been given the opportunity to better himself with such education as was available and how he had the opportunity to earn his own freedom, which, as a matter of fact, he had almost accomplished through the manumittal agreement.

Jack held in his breast a burning desire for freedom, but his desire went further than his own personal affairs. He wanted freedom for his country also. When he had earned his own freedom, he wanted it to be a freedom in a free land where every man is as good as every other man. He wanted to be truly free.

This slave, this Currituck Jack, was in his own way as much a patriot as any man who ever lived. With a wisdom beyond his years and an insight that transcended his times, he decided to stick with his friends and his adopted country.

Jack didn't let his captors know his decision, however. He told them that he would seriously consider their suggestion and would pray over it and let them have his answer before they reached the port of New York.

In belated concern for his health and to show their "sympathy" for him, the prize crew moved Jack that afternoon back down into the dry darkness of the hold where his two shipmates were being held. They tied him tightly even then and secured the hatch as tightly as they could. After all, a slave dead from exposure would bring them no profit in the slave market.

There in the darkness the three friends began to discuss their condition. Jack told the others of the pressures put upon him to defect and join the British and how he had told them he would let them know his answer soon.

The shipmates agreed that therein lay their best and possibly their only chance to recapture the *Polly*. It was agreed among them that Jack would pretend to go over to the British and would offer to help them work the ship as they proceeded northward. Once he gained his freedom he was to look for a chance to free his comrades and join with them in an effort to recapture the *Polly*.

Their decision was made. For warmth, the three Currituck County men lay down as close to each other as their bonds would allow, and they fell into a fitful sleep. They needed their strength for the fight to regain their ship. If they died in the attempt, they would die with honor.

Even Captain Caleb White, devout Quaker that he was, was in complete agreement with the plan, although he hoped in his heart of hearts that there would be no fatalities. His mind was filled with admiration for Jack and the tremendous courage the young man had shown. He had always been fond of the huge black. Now he was more than proud to be associated with him in this daring undertaking.

By the next morning, Jack was burning up with fever. His day and night of exposure to the cruel elements as he lay tied to the deck of the *Polly* was beginning to take its toll. There were times when he was incoherent and other times when he was completely out of his head. In between times, though, he had periods when he was rational, and he insisted on going through with the plan. There was a calculated risk as to whether he would unintentionally reveal the plan in a moment of delirium.

When the prisoners were brought their breakfast, Jack asked

to be taken to see the midshipman who was in charge of the prize crew. He was able to convince the British seaman that he had seen the light and had finally realized that his own best interest lay in siding with the British in exchange for his freedom.

So convincing was Jack and so sincere did he seem that the midshipman ordered him released from his bonds and allowed the freedom of the ship. If he mistook the light of fever in Jack's eyes for fervor for the British cause, no one can blame him. After all, Jack put on a wonderful and convincing show. He repeated all the arguments his captors had made to him.

That very day the storm began to abate and the wind began to subside. Plans were made to get under way the next morning. The prize crew gave Jack the task of carrying the food to his former shipmates in the hope that he could induce them to defect along with him. It was on one of these trips into the hold that he was able to slip Captain Caleb a sharp knife the slave had taken from the galley. Also on that trip he managed to leave the hasp securing the hatch unfastened so that it could be raised from underneath. Jack, you see, had now become one of the prize crew and was allowed to sleep in the cabin.

At dawn the following day, the weather had abated still more. Although a large sea was still running, conditions looked good for resuming the voyage of the *Polly*. During the night, the prisoners belowdecks had used the knife to good effect, both in cutting the ropes that bound them and in picking the locks of the irons in which they had been placed. The hour for action had arrived.

Overhead, the patter of feet on the deck was unmistakable as the prize crew went about weighing the sea anchor and bending sails onto the yards. Captain Caleb and Sam felt the difference in the roll and pitch of their ship, and they knew she was beginning to come under control of her wheel and the pull of the sails, which were being hoisted. Now, if ever, was the time. Now, while all hands were busy bringing the schooner on course.

With all their combined strength, Caleb and Sam managed to throw back the hatch cover onto the deck from beneath, and they came leaping up to the deck. Caleb made straight for the wheel, where the midshipman was trying to bring the schooner onto her assigned course and was fighting the big wheel with all his might. Without more ado, Caleb hung a roundhouse swing flush onto the jaw of the youngster. His blow had all the desperation of a man fighting for everything he held dear. Caught completely by surprise, the midshipman went down and out like a light.

Simultaneously, Jack seized a marlinespike from the fife rail at the mast and lit into the two shipmates who had been helping him raise the bulky mainsail. In a matter of seconds, the two heads were laid open to the skulls and the two figures lay writhing on the deck.

In a perfectly coordinated move, Sam attacked the sailor who, far out on the jib boom, had been attempting to free the outermost jib. Climbing out after the Britisher, Sam wrapped his legs around the jib boom just abaft the dolphin striker and applied a stranglehold with his arms wrapped around the neck of the astounded sailor. He pressed the sailor's head up and against the jib boom until he felt the form grow limp in his grasp. Then, instead of just letting the body drop into the sea, Sam laboriously inched his way back down the jib boom, dragging the limp body of the crewman with him until he reached the deck. Throwing him into the scuppers, Sam then turned to assist Caleb, who was struggling with another member of the prize crew.

The surprise was complete. The Englishmen, very much the worse for wear, were herded by Jack, brandishing a bloody marlinespike, until they were all confined belowdecks in the very forward hold that had been the prison of the Americans. Needless to say, they were all securely tied up, and the hatch cover was double-checked to see that it offered no opportunity for opening from beneath.

Back in control of his ship, Captain Caleb White ordered the British flag taken down and safely stowed in the cabin.

Knowing that they could not possibly reach Boston with Jack as ill as he was, Caleb ordered him belowdecks to the cabin and to bed while the *Polly* was put on a course that soon brought her to a safe anchorage at Annapolis, Maryland.

By that time, Jack was completely out of his head from pneumonia and frostbite from his long exposure. He was tenderly carried ashore, and arrangements were made to have him admitted to the hospital at Annapolis, where he lingered between life and death for several weeks.

Finally, however, his magnificent physical strength began to assert itself, and under the care of doctors, he regained his right senses. More than a month later, he was dismissed to go home.

Meanwhile, the Continental Congress, hearing of Jack's bravery and self-sacrifice, passed a resolution expressing its appreciation and its admiration for his bravery. It even asked that he be made evermore a free and independent citizen of the country he loved so much.

Tradition tells us that, upon his return to Currituck County, Jack not only was freed and made a citizen of his state and country but was given all the money that had accumulated over the years in his manumittal fund.

Tradition also tells us that he used this money to buy the freedom of a very pretty and wholesome black girl whom he had long admired. After he freed her, he married her and settled down with his own boat and his own nets and his own small farm in his beloved Currituck County.

The old folks in the area still talk about Currituck Jack. When some youngster gets overly proud of his strength or his speed or his bravery, the oldsters will tell him the tale of Currituck Jack and how he was not only a physical giant but a gentle and brave American patriot as well.

Currituck Jack is a true and genuine folk hero to the people of our coastland. In the minds of many, he was also one of the finest and least-heralded patriots of our young country.

The Holy Ghost Shell

from *Outer Banks Tales to Remember*

For literally hundreds of years, beachcombing and shell collecting have been pleasant hobbies for both visitors and permanent residents of North Carolina's Outer Banks. Children and adults alike enjoy searching for the beautiful shells found in abundance on the seashore. Some people have amassed large collections. There are even shops that specialize in nothing but shells, both local and foreign.

One of the most popular of these shells is known as the sand dollar. Circular in shape and of various sizes, this skeleton of a small marine animal bleaches out to a pleasing whiteness on the beach and makes an interesting decoration or conversation piece. In the old days they were quite easy to find, but with the advent of millions of tourists and surf fishermen, they are becoming harder and harder to come by. It is now a fairly rare occurrence to find a perfect and unbroken sand dollar on the beach.

Most beach visitors know the sand dollar, but many of them have never heard the legend of that particular seashell, a legend that dates back to the early beginnings of English efforts to colonize this "goodliest soile under the cope of heaven."

When Amadas and Barlowe were sent to explore the land in April of 1584, they brought with them a sizable force of Englishmen to conduct the exploration. It is said that one of the sailors was a man named Henry Fowlkes who was, by nature, of a religious bent. He had even studied to be a priest in the newly formed Anglican Church.

Fowlkes was much impressed with the beauty of the land he was visiting, and he loved to take long, solitary walks along the golden beaches to meditate and to commune with his God. The local Indians were quite friendly and he had no fear of them, but he did not know that the Outer Banks, even then, were visited by upland tribes for the wonderful hunting and fishing they knew they would find. Some of these visitors came from the Iroquoian tribes far to the west, and they were much more warlike and fierce than the local Algonquins. As luck would have it, Fowlkes happened one day on one of these hunting parties and was promptly taken prisoner.

When the hunting party returned to their own village, they took the Englishman with them, and there he remained as a slave, as spring and summer faded into fall and winter. In time he learned the Iroquoian language and taught some of them to speak English, but he was looked down upon as a "squaw man," who was relegated to the most menial tasks and who could expect nothing but contempt.

After he taught them his language, the Englishman began to teach the tribe about Jesus and about his coming to save all mankind, including the Indians. He told them of the crucifixion and the resurrection of the Savior. As his lessons progressed his audience became larger and larger. Some of the women began to inquire how they too could secure this salvation and life eternal. Even the fierce braves began to be interested and to ask searching questions.

The medicine men were infuriated. They saw a threat in this Englishman and his new religion. They greatly feared that their influence would fade away if the Indians accepted Christianity. These ritualists were men of considerable power in the tribe. Using the threat of vengeance by the forest spirits if these teachings were allowed to continue, they persuaded the chiefs to sentence Fowlkes to death for heresy. They insisted that he be taken back to the spot where he had been captured and there be beaten to death with their ceremonial clubs.

Accordingly, in the month of April in the year 1585, a party of braves carried the slave back to the very spot on the beach where he had been found. He was made to kneel in the wet sand, and the medicine men gathered around with their clubs, waiting for the Indian king to strike the first blow.

"Now, white man," intoned the king, "your God and your Jesus-brave know where to find you. Your Holy Ghost must know that this is the spot from which we took you. Call on your gods, and if they are as powerful as you say, ask them for a sign. Give us a sign from nature as our Great Spirit does for us when we pray. Do this and we will release you. Pray, bearded-face! Pray for a sign or you die!"

Believing that death was imminent, Fowlkes clasped his hands and prayed with all his might that he be delivered from dying on this foreign shore, never to see his beloved England again. He was man enough and Christian enough to conclude his prayer with the very words of our Savior, "Father, if it be thy will, let this cup pass from me. Nevertheless, not my will but thine be done."

Snarling, a medicine man kicked the kneeling slave in the face and sent him sprawling into the sand. "He speaks of a cup," sneered the Indian. "Let him drink from the cup of death."

As he struggled to rise from the sand, Fowlkes' hand closed around a large sand dollar. He had not seen such a seashell before, as they are common only on the sandy beaches of North America. He gazed upon it with awe.

"See, see," he shouted, holding the shell up before the chief's face. "Here is your sign. See how this strange shell shows forth the very things I told you about my Lord. See the circular shape like the crown of thorns. See the five slashes—they represent the thorns that pierced His brow. See the five marks in the center of the shell, which show the five wounds my Savior received on the cross. Here is your sign. Only see. See and believe!"

Taking the shell in his trembling hands, the chief turned it over and over and examined it from every angle. As a frequenter of this coast he had seen many of these shells and had wondered about the markings but had never had anyone try to explain them to him. Here, indeed, was the "sign from nature" he demanded of the white man.

The head shaman was staring open-mouthed in amazement, not knowing what to say. The chief turned to hand him the shell, and in the exchange between the hands of the two, the fragile shell broke in half. Out fell several little things that looked exactly like little white doves.

"There is the sign of the Holy Ghost," exulted the prisoner. "This is not the Holy Ghost itself but is a sign—a sign using the image of that same white dove that descended bringing the Comforter to the people until my Lord's coming again."

The legend concludes that the tribesmen then turned and fled the beach and returned with all haste to their village, leaving the Englishman alone upon the strand. It is also said that this may be one explanation of the smattering of Christianity that the early settlers found extant among the inland Indians.

Fowlkes lost no time in walking down the beach to a point opposite Roanoke Island, where he found, to his joy, that Sir Richard Grenville had just arrived with some 600 men and would soon return to England. Sir Richard welcomed Henry Fowlkes as an additional hand on board one of his ships and carried him back to his native land, where Fowlkes entered the Anglican priesthood and spent the rest of his life serving churches in Devon and Yorkshire. He is said to have carried many sand dollars with him and to have used them in his sermons.

Now, you may know that the sand dollars found on the Atlantic and Pacific shores of this country are really specimens of the various thin, circular echinoderms of the order *Clypeastrina*, especially *Echinarachnius parma*, of sandy ocean bottoms of the northern Atlantic and Pacific. But ask any knowledgeable coastal child what one is, and like a little cherub, he will explain to you that it is really the Holy Ghost shell and that his grandfather has shown him the marks of the thorns and wounds. If it is a whole shell, he might break it in two for you and let you see the little snow-white doves that come from the inside.

Imagery? Superstition? Well, now, don't be too sure. "There are more things in this world than are dreamed of in your philosophy."

The Beckoning Hands

from *Outer Banks Mysteries & Seaside Stories*

The basins of the Roanoke and Chowan Rivers were two of the earliest centers of civilization in the New World. Many beautiful homes were built along their shores, and towns such as Plymouth and Edenton played an important part in the settling of the Province of Carolina, both under the Lords Proprietors and under the royal governors.

Most of the mansions built along the lovely shorelines were the creations of planters and import merchants, but at least one was built at the direction of a famous pirate who wanted not only a secure place to keep his plunder, but also a comfortable and gracious showplace where his noble friends—governors and statesmen and such—could be entertained in the gracious style to which they were accustomed. After all, he considered himself a sort of import merchant, too. You see, even in those days it was not unusual for some of the more successful criminals to want to cross the line into respectability for themselves and their families.

The edifice of which we speak is still standing on the top of a small but high bluff overlooking the Chowan River. It was carefully planned down to the last cubic foot. Its masonry walls are very thick, almost like a fort, making it nearly soundproof and very easy to heat in winter and cool in summer. A large basement gives opening to a brick-lined tunnel that descends through the heart of the bluff to a well-concealed door at the level of the river.

This made the unloading of boats a very practical matter, as well as a very private one. No prying eye could possibly see what was being transferred from rowboats to the mouth of the tunnel or vice versa.

The high ground upon which the house is located afforded an excellent lookout both up and down the river, so the occupants had ample notice of the approach of any travelers by water and could take any steps they considered expedient. As most travel in those days was by boat, the beautiful home was indeed a very snug and secure nest.

At the will of the owner, the splendid structure could be either a fort or a gracious palace. It was built by the most skillful artisans and of only the very best materials obtainable from the seven seas of the world. In addition to the stones of which the basic structure was built, there were rosewood, mahogany, and teakwood from the tropics and golden oak from the timbers of captured ships. The house was built with all the meticulous attention to detail and strength that the skilled boatwright is accustomed to putting into the building of an ocean-going vessel. It is still sound and secure down to this very day.

Perhaps the most striking feature of the interior of the mansion was the grand entrance. Here a huge hall was lighted by sterling silver sconces bearing wax candles that blazed brilliantly. A very wide staircase opened just opposite the massive front doors. Made of highly polished mahogany, the staircase swept upward in a graceful flair and opened on an upstairs hall, which served as a passageway to the rooms of the upper floors. Carpeted with fabulous oriental rugs, the hall and stair gave dramatic welcome to the house as one entered the front doors. The rugs are no longer there, but that magnificent staircase still sweeps in its graceful and imposing curve, inviting the guest to enter and explore the regions above.

Large parlors and dining rooms open off this large entrance hall, and in its early days a kitchen was located to the rear of the house, providing easy and direct access to the dining room through a butler's pantry.

The only trouble was that the family of the would-be-respectable pirate would never live there with him.

His lovely young wife did not approve of his piratical ways nor of his affairs with other ladies of the area. But she was also apprehensive about a curse that had been laid on her pirate husband by an old hag who lived in Nags Head Woods.

It seems he had "pressed" or kidnapped the old woman's son, an only child, into service aboard the pirate ship. The boy had subsequently been killed during an attack upon a merchant ship, and the old crone blamed the pirate captain for depriving her of any hope of grandchildren. In spite of a rather large sum of money given to her by the buccaneer, she swore a curse on his head to the effect that he, too, should never know the joy of being a grandparent, but that his line should be cut off for all time and forever.

It was shortly after news of this malediction reached her that the brigand's wife left him and took their daughter back to her home town of Charleston, South Carolina. She maintained separate quarters in a lovely house there, and the pirate was free to visit her and their beautiful young daughter Caroline.

Several years later, the pirate captain caught a fever in the West Indies and died aboard ship. He was buried at sea according to the custom of the Brotherhood of the Sea, and his faithful first mate then sailed openly into Charleston harbor to carry the news of his passing to his widow. He also carried his captain's sword, other personal belongings, and the shipmaster's share of the accumulated loot, which amounted, in value, to a sizable sum. This, together with her other holdings and previous gifts from her husband, left the widow quite comfortably fixed.

Among the properties inherited by the widow and her daughter was the beautiful mansion overlooking the river, and the two of them soon took up residence there. It was much cooler in the summers, and the winters did not seem to be as piercingly cold or damp. The house was magnificently appointed and very comfortable, and the neighbors on adjoining plantations were what was termed "quality folk." All in all, it seemed a nearly ideal place to complete the rearing of a daughter.

Caroline grew in grace and in beauty and soon was the toast of the entire region. The great stone house often rang with music and merriment as the young folk of the province gathered for extended homeparties that lasted several days at the very least. Life was pleasant, unhurried, and serene. There was plenty of delicious food, plenty of good and genteel company, plenty of light and laughter, and above all, plenty of time in which to live the good life to the fullest.

Or so they thought.

Youth and laughter and friendship blossomed into love for the beautiful, diminutive Caroline, and wedding arrangements were soon made for her marriage to the scion of one of the oldest and wealthiest families in the entire Roanoke-Chowan area.

The wedding ceremony was to take place at the home of the bride, and invitations went out to all the great and many of the near-great in that whole region. It was to be a brilliant social affair, with the ceremony to be performed by a visiting bishop of the Anglican Church. The house was beautifully decorated with Christmas decorations, for the ceremony was to take place on New Year's Day, still a part of the Christmas season. A string orchestra was brought in from Edenton to furnish the wedding music, and the days preceding New Year's were an endless round of parties and holiday festivities.

The wedding day arrived at last. The Bishop made an imposing figure in his vestments as he stood very erect, prayer book in hand, ready to perform the nuptial ceremony. He and all the other guests were assembled in the great hall. The nervous young bridegroom was in his place beside the Bishop, and the bride was to enter from a dressing room located just off the great hall.

The orchestra struck up the wedding music, played it once, then again, but the bride did not appear. The Bishop cleared his throat and glanced over at the mother of the bride, who was beginning to experience the first symptoms of panic. A chill of premonition gripped her, and she remembered the curse of the Nags Head hag.

Then, from above the level of their heads, came . . . a very feminine giggle!

All eyes snapped immediately to the head of the huge stairway, and there they beheld the bride in all her wedding finery, looking down at them with twinkling eyes and with a teasing smile on her pretty lips. She looked no bigger than a child as she stood there, radiantly happy and the most beautiful thing the bridegroom had ever seen. In spite of warnings that he must not look upon his bride in her wedding dress until she stood beside him at the altar, the young man could not take his eyes off her.

Tiny Caroline stood there for a brief moment, poised like a bird. She was reveling in the adoration and adulation flowing toward her from her beloved and her friends on the floor below.

Then, with an impish grin and looking directly into the eyes of her fiancé, she taunted, "Catch me and you may kiss me." She tossed her pretty, lace-bedecked head and beckoned to him with both her hands. Turning, she ran swiftly along the upstairs hall and disappeared around a corner.

Accepting the challenge, the young bridegroom leaped forward and ran up the broad stairway, three steps at a time, until he reached the hall above. Then he turned in the direction his beloved had taken and ran down the hallway after her.

There was no Caroline!

Up and down the halls he ran and into all the rooms, and still he could not find his bride. Calling her, he begged her to come out of her hiding place, as the wedding guests were becoming restless and the Bishop was distinctly annoyed at this frivolous interruption of the religious ceremony.

Soon amusement or annoyance turned into genuine concern as the whole wedding party joined in the search for the missing girl. The great stone house was searched thoroughly, and the grounds around the house were carefully explored for hundreds of yards, but without producing a sign of the young girl. No strangers had been seen in the vicinity, and there was no known wild beast thereabouts that was large enough to have carried her off. No boats were missing from any of the piers along the waterfront.

Caroline had just disappeared without a trace.

After several months of futile search, Caroline's bereaved mother closed up the big stone house and moved away. It is said that the mysterious disappearance of her lovely daughter continued to grieve her and stayed on her mind so much that she soon became deranged and would talk of nothing but her lost bride-girl. There is no doubt that her grief shortened her life. The poor, troubled lady died without ever finding out what had become of Caroline.

The very next New Year's night, one year to the day after the strange disappearance, some children in the neighborhood of the great stone house came home badly frightened and told their parents of seeing a ghostly, white face floating and flitting from window to window inside the closed mansion. They said the "thing" beckoned enticingly with two ghostly, white hands. Their frightened parents forbade them to go ever again upon the grounds of the old pirate's mansion. Of course, being children, they did go back, but none of them was ever harmed.

Year after year, always on New Year's night, the pallid face and beckoning hands continued to appear in the windows of the house until the ghost became a local and then a regional attraction. Many brave people tried to solve the mystery of the apparition, but when they gained admittance to the house, the phenomenon always vanished with a long and pitiful sigh.

The old pirate's beautiful home became known as "the house with the beckoning hands," and prudent people avoided it whenever they could. Nevertheless, many upright and reliable people—people of unquestioned sobriety—swore that they continued to see those beckoning hands and that pitiful face, but no one could solve the mystery.

Then, years later, a man who had made a deep study of such things rented the house from its owners to try to get to the bottom of the strange occurrence. Many believed he was a little touched in the head to be searching for a solution to a mystery that had gone unexplained all those years.

He actually moved into the house to try to obtain, first-hand, the feeling and the mood of the place. All by himself, he searched the house from top to bottom again and again. He never actually saw the beckoning hands or the wistful face, but he was convinced that his neighbors were telling the truth.

Then, on New Year's night, after he had waited in vain for the apparition, he fell asleep in the huge feather bed in the master bedroom of the house. As he slept he dreamed a very vivid dream.

He dreamed that he was witnessing that strange, interrupted wedding ceremony of many years before. He saw all the actors in the event as though from a vantage point above and beyond the wedding party, so he could see all of them at one time.

In his dream he saw the bridegroom leaping up the stairs in pursuit of his young, lovely bride, and he saw tiny Caroline turn and run down the hall in mock fright from her beloved.

And then he saw it. As Caroline dashed along the hall and turned a corner, she lost her balance in her long wedding dress and fell against the wall for support. Her steadying hand reached into a secret crevice in that stone wall and touched a secret lever. He saw a trapdoor open beneath her feet, and he caught a flash of wedding finery as she fell through that trapdoor and into a secret, windowless room beneath. He saw the trapdoor reclose as the heavy stone flooring turned upon its metal pivot and glided into place, locking shut with a metallic click.

In his dream, Caroline was entombed alive! The sheer horror of his vivid dream shocked him into consciousness, and he awoke with a scream.

Did his ears betray him or did he hear the high-pitched cackle of an old hag? As he rolled from his bed, the first light of a winter dawn was breaking over the eastern sky.

Without more ado, but trembling as if he had an ague, our

researcher went directly to that portion of the hall he had seen so clearly in his dream. The stone wall was still there, and so was that secret crack or joint between the stones. Pushing his hand wrist-deep into the aperture, he felt the end of a rusty metal lever which, with great exertion, he was able to move.

Slowly, slowly, and with a great groaning sound as though it were reluctant to reveal its secret, the huge stone in the floor began to swing on its now rusty pivot until it stood fully open. A vagrant beam of sunlight fell directly into the opening before him.

There, on the floor of that secret room, he beheld a tiny human skeleton, almost as small as a child's, the bones of both hands extended along the floor in a beckoning gesture. On the head of the skeleton there was a trace of ancient white lace, almost like snow upon its brow. The wedding veil of lovely Caroline.

And thus was the mystery finally solved. The remains of poor Caroline were given Christian burial, and the treacherous trapdoor was sealed shut so that it could never again imprison an unsuspecting traveler along that hallway.

The beckoning hands?

Well, most of the people in the neighborhood will tell you that they disappeared from that day on, but there are others who will tell you that they can still be seen, but only on a dark New Year's night. They are beckoning, ever beckoning.

The Female of the Species

from *The Flaming Ship of Ocracoke & Other Tales of the Outer Banks*

In the early days of this country, North Carolina's coastal region was the main theater of operations for many a well-known pirate. Some, like the famous Blackbeard, were admired and looked up to as heroes by the poorer settlers. Others were greatly feared because of their reputations for cruelty and sadism. But none of this motley "Brotherhood of the Sea" were quite so colorful as the two famous female pirates of the day, Anne Bonny and Mary Read. Each was, in a sense, a product of coastal Carolina in the early days of colonization.

Anne Bonny was born in County Cork, Ireland, the illegitimate daughter of a wealthy lawyer and his wife's maid. Because of some trouble, possibly political in nature, Bonny and the maid took Anne and fled across the Atlantic to the New World, leaving his wife in Ireland.

When they arrived, Bonny purchased an extensive estate on the beautiful, broad waters of the Neuse River just below

New Berne in what is now Craven County, and he prospered from the start. He was industrious as well as highly intelligent, so he soon achieved considerable status as a lawyer, merchant, and farmer. Much of his business was in trading with the many ships that plied the Neuse River from the nearby Atlantic sea lanes. He even seemed to have mended his political fortunes to the point where he became magistrate, and his beautiful home became one of the showplaces of the area in which he lived.

When Anne's mother died, the girl naturally moved into her place as mistress of the household, directing the several servants who were apprenticed or "bound" to the place in exchange for having been given free passage to the new land of opportunity. Whether it was the lack of maternal supervision and loss of the softening effect of a mother's love or whether it was just Anne's basic nature coming to the surface will never be known, but the girl soon developed into a self-centered, strong-willed tyrant in her own little sphere. She brooked absolutely no opposition to her will. She lorded her authority over the women servants, in particular, and missed no opportunity to vent her spite on anyone she considered beneath her.

According to contemporary accounts of the times, Anne Bonny, even as a girl, possessed "a fierce and courageous" temper, which she took little pains to conceal. Reliable local tradition insists that, when a frightened maidservant once accidentally spilled hot soup over one of her favorite dinner gowns, the enraged Anne sprang from her seat, seized one of the dirks lying on a nearby mantel, and disemboweled the luckless maid with one savage, twisting slash. Squire Bonny was finally able to hush up the killing by the judicious use of a considerable amount of his wealth, but Anne's reputation spread about the countryside like wildfire.

In spite of her reputation for cruelty, Anne had many suitors among the local gentry. Although she was known to be of a violent disposition, she was also the only child of a very wealthy father. It was presumed that she would someday inherit all of the family possessions. Besides, man has always toyed with the idea that he could somehow succeed in taming the shrew, even though others before him had failed.

And what a shrew for the taming Anne was! Tall for a woman and almost manly in her movements, she was, nevertheless, wide-hipped and deep-bosomed, broad of shoulder and strong of thigh, a veritable Amazon. A wild sort of beauty she had, with a wealth of shining, jet-black hair and large, flashing blue eyes betokening a spirit that no man had ever been able to tame. She was a superb horsewoman and an expert in the use of sword and pistol, the result of patient training by her doting, though sometimes bewildered father.

This was the prize contended for by many of the young Carolinians who lived thereabout. Although they all professed undying affection and desire for her, and although several even went so far as to fight duels over her, she treated them all with amused contempt. "Milksops," she called them, "pretty boys," and "fortune hunters." She was the ultimate challenge to every mother's son of them, and they resented her cool disdain.

Considering her poor opinion of most men, the manner of her falling in love was most unusual. On her part, it was love at first sight, and the object of her affection was a plain, ordinary sailor from one of the merchant ships that had called at her father's wharf. He was a reformed pirate who had taken the King's Pardon, and he owned nothing in this world but the marlinespike stuck in his belt and the sailor's clothes he stood in. But he was young, healthy, and handsome, and Anne was very much taken with him. Who can say what magic or what chemistry first attracts a maid to a man? At first he ran like a scared rabbit from Anne's bold, open approach. He had never seen a woman like her. His shipmates soon pointed out to him the many advantages of a rich wife such as Squire Bonny's daughter. Thereafter, the courtship moved at a goodly pace with overtures on both sides.

When the day came they were sure they could no longer go on without each other, the young couple went to John Bonny and asked his permission to marry. At this preposterous request, all the pent-up worry and frustration this Irish gentleman felt about his daughter broke loose. His hitherto repressed Irish temper flared into full flame. In no uncertain terms, he denied their request and ordered the young sailor off his premises, never to return on threat of violent death. Shouting imprecations at the top of his voice against penniless fortune hunters, he ordered his daughter to her room to stay until he gave her leave to come forth. Then, pistol in hand, he escorted the terrified suitor back to his vessel and aided his ascent of the gangplank with a mighty kick.

Alas for Squire Bonny! Did he really think that he could thus thwart either true love or the iron will of his daughter? Even as the elder Bonny proceeded to quench the heat of his anger by drinking himself into oblivion, Anne busied herself upstairs gathering up all the money and other valuables she could lay her hands on. Having collected a considerable sum, she silently escaped down the roof which slanted gently almost to the ground outside her bedroom window. She then quietly made her way to her lover's ship which, under orders of the Squire, was even then preparing to cast off and be on its way.

By spending only a small part of her valuables, Anne was able to persuade the captain to alter his plans and to take them down the Neuse River and through the ancient thoroughfare by Cedar Island to Beaufort Town, where they were married in the little chapel. In Beaufort, she purchased a small but strong coastal schooner with the remainder of her dower wealth. While the little schooner was being outfitted and loaded with cargo, the honeymooning couple spent a few happy weeks at a combined inn and tavern in Beaufort called the Inn of the Three Horseshoes, a fairly new hostelry operated by a man named Jack Read and his young wife of a few months, Mary. It was a happy time, and it seemed that the very name of the inn presaged a bright future for the young couple. The elder Bonny did not put in an appearance to mar their happiness. The Inn of the Three Horseshoes became their first home, and each of them felt that nothing could possibly arise to threaten their happiness.

At last all was ready. Their graceful little ship was completely fitted out for sea and held a cargo of tobacco and naval stores consigned for delivery in Boston. Although it has always been a tradition of the sea that it is bad luck to have any woman aboard ship, Anne could not bring herself to part with her new husband, so she sailed with him on the first voyage of the new ship.

On a bright and sparkling day, the little schooner took advantage of a tide just past its peak and sailed smartly out of Beaufort Harbor, around Shark Shoal, and out the inlet into the blue-green Atlantic. The crewmen, who had been hired in Beaufort Town, seemed to know their duties. They handled the sails and the rigging smartly as the bridegroom leaned expertly against the mahogany wheel, his radiant bride reclining gracefully against the lee rail of the afterdeck.

As the sails bellied taut with the favorable breeze and the immortal song of the sea began to sing from the forefoot and along the water line of the little craft, everything seemed almost too perfect. Little did Anne know, nor could she tell, the horror that awaited them just over the horizon. The fate that now hurried toward them was destined so to change her entire life that her name would go down in history, alongside that of the infamous Lucrezia Borgia of Italy, as one of the most cruel and bloodthirsty female creatures known to the memory of man. In that hour of beginnings, though, no shadow of impending fate spoiled the mood of the travelers as they cleared Beaufort Inlet and set their course to join the Gulf Stream as it swept northward toward Diamond Shoals. Every prospect was auspicious, and hearts were high.

About midafternoon of the second day out, as the Bight of Hatteras came into view, a lively brigantine burst into sight, racing from behind the cape point before the gentle northeast breeze. Every square sail of her, from the big mainsail right on up to the topgallant sails, was drawing beautifully.

Few sights are more beautiful than that of a sailing ship handled as she should be handled and sailed right up to the full of her potential. But the honeymooners scarcely had time to catch their breath in appreciation of this beautiful scene before they saw another detail which caused their blood to run cold. Atop the mainmast, just above the straining, white topgallant sail, was a huge rectangular, black flag bearing the outline in red of a human skeleton. The very worst had befallen the bride and groom. Here was the greatest danger they could have encountered, the pirate ship *Fancy* under the command of the mad Captain Edward Low. Low was known the seven seas over as an insane seafaring genius, whose chief delight was inflicting torture and slow death on each member of the luckless crews of the ships he captured.

Early in his piratical career, the left side of Low's face had been laid open to the bone and teeth by the vicious sabre slash of an adversary. After the battle, the ship's surgeon had tried in vain to sew up the ugly wound. The pirate, by then roaring drunk as the result of his efforts to find both an antiseptic and an anesthetic in the rum bottle, would not lie still. Crazy with pain and rum, he knocked the surgeon senseless and tried to sew up his own face with the curved needle. He made such a mess of it that, forever after, his head resembled the caricature of a skull. The yellowed teeth and bone shone through the slit cheek in a horrible grimace even when his face was relaxed, giving him an expression of deadly menace.

There seems to be no doubt at all that the pirate captain was violently insane. Consequently, he was one of the most dreaded robbers and murderers who roved the sea lanes of that day. The very sight of his red skeleton flag struck terror to the hearts of most seafarers. It is said that this capacity to terrify his victims often resulted in the abject surrender of many vessels to his flag without any fight whatsoever.

Now, Anne Bonny's new husband was no fool. He knew instantly that their only hope lay in precipitate flight, and he and his little crew very smartly "wore ship" and fled in the opposite direction in a desperate effort to run into shallower water over some nearby shoals. The brigantine was the larger and faster ship, however, and she already had considerable momentum or "way" on. The pursuit turned out to be no race.

Before the fascinated gaze of a score of natives on the shore, the *Fancy* cut off the little schooner from the shoal, came alongside, threw huge grappling hooks over her rail, and proceeded to send a boarding party onto her decks. When the brief resistance of the crew was overcome and the two ships were firmly lashed together, the mad captain himself boarded Anne's vessel.

The scene of human torture that followed is better left undescribed, although the descendants of those on shore talk about it to this day. Anne Bonny was stripped to the waist and tied securely to the mast of her ship. She was the butt of many an obscene and cruel jest as the pirates forced her to look on, during intermittent periods of consciousness, while the surviving crewmen and her husband were slowly and brutally killed. As the frightened and horrified fisherman on the island watched from hiding in the yaupon and scrub cedar, the lifeless bodies of the crew were thrown over the rail into the midst of an increasing number of sharks, which were attracted by the scent of blood in the water.

Anne's little vessel was looted, stripped of her running rigging and fittings, and set afire to burn and drift with the tide. Anne herself was taken prisoner aboard the pirate ship, which soon thereafter returned to that nest of pirates known as the island of New Providence in the Bahamas.

This lovely island contained a most amazing government of, by, and for pirates. The Brotherhood of the Sea maintained some semblance of order in disorder. There were fights and duels aplenty among individual freebooters, but strict loyalty was maintained to the charter of the place. Each ship's company was a little community within the general community, and each captain was responsible for the conduct of his men. In disputes between crews, a jury from the crews of other ships was hastily summoned to sit in judgment. Strangely enough, a rough sort of justice was achieved, and there was little quarreling with the decisions of the juries. Only the captain of a ship could pass judgment of death upon one of his crew, and that only with the agreement of a majority of the sailors on that particular ship. The division of the spoils between individual crew members was decided by a strict formula to which all ships adhered, and a percentage of the loot was paid to maintain the stronghold.

Released ashore on New Providence as a free woman and left to perish or survive by her own wits, Anne soon became a well-known figure in the community. Although many people believe she never fully regained her right mind after the massacre off Hatteras, her will to live was strong. Anne not only subsisted; she also became one of the favorites of the pirate captains for whom New Providence was the nearest thing to a home they ever knew. The island itself possessed a spirit, a sort of flavor, that was not entirely disagreeable to the wild, boisterous spirit of Anne Bonny. Here she found men who could match her own cruelty. They were her equals in physical bravery, and they lived and died with a swagger and an *élan* that she found completely fascinating and often admirable.

One of the moving spirits in this den of buccaneers was a worthy named John James Rackham. It was this same Rackham who connived with the famous Blackbeard to maroon the pirate Captain Charles Vane on a lonely island so that Rackham, Vane's former mate, could steal Vane's ship and sail in convoy with Blackbeard. Honor among thieves? Well, Rackham's outwitting of Captain Vane was related with shouts of laughter all over the pirate world, and the trickster was thereby enabled to cut quite a figure in that lawless society. After obtaining command of his own ship in this doubly piratical way, Rackham began to affect britches made of bright calico cloth. These became his trademark, and he soon became known as "Calico Jack" Rackham.

Anne Bonny and Calico Jack were attracted to each other from the very first. Anne was growing weary of the humdrum life ashore, and one of the conditions she interposed when Calico Jack proposed marriage was that he take her with him whenever he went a-pirating.

It was unclear whether any person even remotely connected with the church was present at the pirate wedding, but a wedding there was. A wilder, more flamboyant and bacchanalian week was never seen, even on the island of New Providence.

Apparently, there were rules and customs that applied to pirate weddings, although they were quite different from those employed under more normal circumstances. The two principals finally stood up and faced each other on the sandy beach and repeated to each other an approximation of the wedding vows. All hands seemed to consider the marriage quite binding, however; from that time forward, it was accepted without question that Calico Jack and Anne were husband and wife.

Rackham kept his prenuptial promise to the letter. Maybe he was afraid not to. Anyway, the arrangement resulted in one of the most fantastic situations imaginable. Anne not only sailed with Rackham on his piratical cruises; she also took delight in donning a man's attire and participating in the actual hand-to-hand fighting and looting with as much gusto as any member of the crew. There were dark mutterings among some members of that crew about defying the ancient taboo against a woman on shipboard. Many were the predictions of disaster sure to follow if the practice was continued.

It had its pleasanter side, though. Anne was a thoroughly dependable and trustworthy ally to have on a boarding party, and the meals she occasionally cooked for the crew were delicious beyond anything they normally had on board ship. Besides, Anne and Calico Jack were without doubt the two most deadly swordsmen in the entire motley aggregation. It could well have cost you your life to give offense to either of them.

Some historians believe that, all this time, Anne was hoping against hope for an encounter with the crazy Captain Edward Low and a chance to even the score with him. He was not a member of the New Providence society, and they never met at sea, so that chance was denied her.

There was one instance and, so far as we know, only one, of near-infidelity to mar this somewhat idyllic, if unlawful, relationship dedicated to violence and crime. Because of the inevitable toll of constant combat, Rackham's crew, at one time, was reduced in number to the point where it was difficult to man the ship in a storm and where the outcome of a battle was becoming more and more doubtful. Being, above all else, a realist, Calico Jack then began to attack somewhat smaller ships and to offer the conquered crewmen of those ships the choice of walking the plank or joining the pirate crew with the promise of a full share of the booty. Understandably, many of those previously honest seamen took the blood oath and joined the Rackham crew, and many of them developed quite an aptitude for piracy and infused new energy into the company.

One such converted merchant seaman was a young sailor who signed in blood with the name "M. Read." Lithe and agile, and with the smooth beardless cheek normally associated with the young, the sunburned youth immediately caught the fancy of Anne Bonny Rackham. There was a gentleness and a grace about this new crew member that stood out in sharp contrast to the bearing of the others. With her accustomed directness and openness, Anne began to pursue and attempt to court, in a hundred different ways, this new object of her fascination. The fact that M. Read seemed to shy away from her and avoid her advances only fanned the flame of her interest and made her redouble her efforts.

The climax of this very one-sided affair occurred one warm, starlit night when the pirate ship was anchored in the natural harbor of a beautiful Caribbean island. Most of the crew had gone ashore with Rackham in search of pigs, which they seized from the natives. The pirates then proceeded to "boucan" the half-wild porkers right there on the beach.

Now, to boucan a pig was the very same thing as barbecuing it, and the result of the boucan was a delicious gustatory treat of which pirates all over that region were very fond. In fact, boucans were so frequent that the pirates eventually became known as "boucan-eers," and this term later became, through much usage, simply "buccaneers." Thus, a buccaneer was a heavily armed sea robber who came ashore on an island, stole the natives' pigs, and barbecued them on the beach. The boucan was usually concluded with a prolonged drinking spree which left senseless and snoring on the sand all but a few assigned to guard the pirate ship.

And so it was on the night of which we speak. Only Anne Bonny and three or four of the crew, M. Read among them, remained on board the ship.

Knowing that M. Read was assigned the anchor watch and was thus unable to leave the deck of the pirate ship, Anne waited until the few members of the crew left aboard had settled down to sleep. All was calm and serene; the moon cast a beautiful glow over the deck, and Anne felt that her golden moment of opportunity was at hand. With a soft fire in her eyes, Anne Bonny moved in for the capture.

Taking a seat beside the handsome, young, smooth-skinned sailor, the ardent lady pirate began to make a complete confession of her feelings for her younger shipmate. Quite eloquently did Anne argue her case, and quite directly and boldly, as was her wont. She was apparently oblivious to the danger that she might be overheard by a wakeful member of the crew and her conduct reported to Rackham.

All this while young Read remained silent, indicating only by an occasional nervous movement of the head or a desperate sidelong glance overside that Anne's words were even heard or, if heard, were making any impression whatsoever. Finally, with a sigh of resignation, young Read turned so that each was looking directly into the other's face and made a disclosure that must have shaken Anne to her very corset stays!

M. Read was a woman, also!

Then, in a veritable torrent of words, Mary Read told how it had come about that she was also dressed in men's clothing and carrying out the duties of a merchant seaman. Now she also became oblivious to the danger of being overheard. Now it was the silent one who felt the compulsion to talk and talk and talk until her full story was known to the other woman sitting there in stunned silence by her side. The tale she told was, if anything, more incredible than Anne Bonny's had been.

Soon after her birth in England, Mary Read's parents had decided to play a trick on her paternal grandmother by concealing the fact that the baby was a girl instead of the male heir the old lady had hopefully expected. Feeling that little Mary would be disinherited if it were learned that she was a girl, the parents did everything in their power to carry out the deception. They dressed her in boys' clothing, gave her the nickname "Jack," and insisted that she learn and practice boys' games and pastimes.

The deceit might have worked with the desired result except for the fact that the old lady lived on and on, and her health got better with age. What had started as a calculated fraud resulted in the development of a muscular, active, and profane counterfeit of a young man of the lower middle class. Grandma really had cause to believe that her grandchild was a virile, strapping young man, and she made occasional generous gifts to this favorite grandchild, but the bulk of her estate she kept in order to see to her own comfort and security.

Bored with her life in England, Mary then decided that, if she was going to have the name of a boy, she might as well have some of the fun boys are supposed to have. She hoped that her grandmother would believe all the more strongly that she was the male heir everyone assumed her to be. Running away from home, the strapping youth enlisted in the infantry in Flanders and served out a full enlistment undetected. Disliking the constant marching, she then shipped out on an English merchant ship and got her first taste of life at sea which, from her standpoint as a cabin "boy," she found less than attractive.

After a year at sea, her ship docked again in Flanders, and she promptly jumped ship and reenlisted in the Flemish armed services, this time in a regiment of cavalry. Then, she felt she was in an occupation that suited her very well. She came to love the thrilling massed charges of the full brigade of horses, the stealthy thrill of picket duty on horseback, and the satisfying sense of being needed as she rubbed down her horse and cared for him and fed him. In those days, the acceptable standards of personal hygiene and sanitation were vastly different from minimum standards today. Even so, it is remarkable that her masquerade could have succeeded as long as it did and that "Jack Hawkins," guidon bearer for a regiment of horse, should have gone so long unrevealed.

In the end, it was her own feminine nature which betrayed her. A dashing, handsome young cavalryman named Jack Read, a man who seemed to epitomize the traits she admired in men, was transferred into her regiment. The better she knew him, the better she liked him. In due course, she confessed both her true sex and her affection for him. Read must have been among the most startled of men. Cavalrymen, however, traditionally have a fine sense of balance, and when he recovered his aplomb, he discovered that he reciprocated Mary's feelings.

Laying their plans well, the two sweethearts deserted their regiment just in time to catch a ship bound for the Carolina colonies. They were married on shipboard by the Captain and traveled finally to Beaufort Town in North Carolina, where they set up a combination inn and tavern. They soon accumulated a fine stable of horses, and, to show their love for things equine, they named their establishment "The Three Horseshoes." It was the very inn at which Anne Bonny and her bridegroom had spent their honeymoon after running away from Anne's father. Now the two women's paths had crossed again, but under what different circumstances!

Mary swore that she remembered Anne and her young husband and that she had remarked, at the time, on what a handsome couple they made. She had not known what had finally become of Anne until the first day she saw her in woman's dress on the pirate ship. From that day on, she had been much too frightened to reveal herself.

Mary Read's husband had died in Beaufort and, for a while, she had operated the Inn of Three Horseshoes by herself. But the work was more than she could handle alone, and the care of several horses was a burden to her. She longed for the old, carefree life of the sea and thought of it more and more often. When she finally had a chance to sell the inn and the horses for a good price, she sold out, lock, stock, and barrel. Traveling to Portsmouth Island, she once again donned the male attire she knew so well and signed on a merchant ship as a seaman. M. Read remained unsuspected and undiscovered until Anne's interest forced her disclosure.

Thereafter, the two women became good friends, and Anne did not betray her new friend's secret until Calico Jack's jealousy made him suspicious of the tanned young sailor with whom Anne was often seen engaging in animated conversation. Poor Rackham! He had no way of knowing that it was only "woman talk" between them, so he confronted the pair one day, dagger in hand, fully prepared to do violence to M. Read. After first swearing him to secrecy, Anne and Mary revealed her secret to the pirate captain. Thunderstruck and speechless in his amazement, Calico Jack could only cover his confusion with roars of laughter.

Rackham kept his vow of secrecy, and M. Read was able to keep her place as a member of the crew, neither asking nor giving favor in the performance of all the tasks involved in the business of sea robbery. Legend has it that Anne Bonny and M. Read frequently engaged in fencing matches with each other and so sharpened their skills with the dirk, the sword, and the pistol that the other crewmen held them, not only in respect, but in absolute fear. They never seemed to quarrel between themselves. Perhaps each had too much respect for the deadly skills of the other, or perhaps there was a bond of sympathy between them.

Mary Read was apparently content to continue her sham and live the life of a pirate crewman on board ship. When the buccaneers went ashore, she could not join fully in the roistering and wild, drunken celebrating that went on. There was too much danger, she thought, that she would inadvertently reveal her true nature. Thus, Mary lived a rather lonely life when all around her were whooping it up, and she began to long, once more, for a more normal, womanly existence, even as a pirate. After all, Anne Bonny was a woman and was accepted without question, in spite of the ancient superstition that a woman was bad luck aboard a ship. But Anne had a husband, and that seemed to make all the difference.

It seemed as though the gods of the sea took pity on Mary's plight. On the very next expedition, Rackham's ship captured a vessel manned by a youngish crew of better than average sailors. Appealing to the pirate captain, Mary chose one of the captured sailors as her full share of the prize. This was sometimes done by pirates who, thenceforward, held these "slaves" as enforced servants until it suited their pleasure to free them, sometimes years later. Mary had other ideas in mind for her prize. Imagine the astonishment of her slave when Mary got him ashore, disclosed her true sex to him and then told him she intended to make him her husband!

History does not tell us what, if any, alternative was offered the young captive, but whatever it was, he chose marriage to Mary Read. From all accounts, this fellow was a gentle, mild sort of person, more given to books and philosophy than to burning and looting. Now Mary considered that she was almost on an equal footing with Anne Bonny Rackham. Now she, too, had a husband.

After her true sex was revealed and accepted as Anne's had been, Mary and her bridegroom were allowed to sign on with Rackham's crew and put to sea with the promise of equal shares in any loot. But trouble developed almost immediately. Another pirate, one of the most hated and feared of the crew, promptly picked a quarrel with the new husband. A challenge to a duel to the death was quickly made and accepted. The alternative would have been a slit throat, but the prospect of a duel itself offered little more hope. Poor Mary! She knew full well that her new mate was no match for the other pirate and would probably be killed in the first passage at arms. If she had no husband, Calico Jack Rackham would probably not want her aboard; her entire piratical career was hanging in the balance.

With characteristic directness, Mary Read confronted her problem. Seeking out the challenging pirate, she demanded words with him. Smirking at what he thought would be her frantic pleas for her husband's life and hurriedly calculating what profit he could make out of the situation, the bully agreed to the conference. How confused he must have been when the first thing the woman did was smack him with her open palm across his bearded face with all her considerable strength. Completely surprised and half blinded by the unexpected blow, the unsuspecting brigand struck back with his fists and, thus, sealed his own doom. Claiming mortal insult, Mary Read challenged him to a duel. Under the rules that governed such affairs at the time, she had the choice of the time and the place for the duel. Now smiling self-confidently, she chose the beach of a nearby island as the place. And the time? She named the time as exactly two hours before the scheduled duel between her husband and that same pirate.

For weapons, the unfortunate brigand chose both swords and pistols in close combat. But his fate was already decided, and he knew it. To his credit be it said that he put up a good fight for a few minutes before Mary Read's skill prevailed. She allowed him the one shot from his pistol, which missed. Then she proceeded to cut him to ribbons before she finally killed him. She wanted to set an example that other would-be challengers of her husband would remember, and she succeeded. Calico Jack sent a burial party ashore, and that was that.

Never again was the set-up challenged, and the reputation of the two married couples mushroomed. The very unnaturalness of the situation sent chills of horror down the spine of many an honest seafarer. Tales of the cruelty and complete lack of pity evidenced by the two women were exaggerated and multiplied time and again. Rumor fed on rumor until the two women were thought to be very fiends of hell itself. This pleased them no end, as it was exactly the impression they wished most to convey.

No matter what their other vices, the two women are said never to have indulged in strong drink, either ashore or afloat. It would have been better for them all if the other pirates had been abstainers too. At least they might have escaped capture longer. As it turned out, a British man-of-war, sent out from Jamaica to look for this very pirate ship, finally located the marauder lying at anchor off a beautiful little Caribbean island. Most of her pirate crew were roaring drunk below decks with only Anne, Mary, and two or three others on deck.

The Britisher came alongside before the pirate could get her anchors up. Grappling irons were thrown over the rail, and a boarding party of British Marines swarmed aboard. Even then the buccaneers might have turned the tide if they had fought back. They heavily outnumbered their attackers and were as skilled in such fighting, but they were in no condition to fight from Rackham on down. The sound of the battle on the decks over their heads struck terror in their drunken brains, and they cowered below in fright as the tide of the battle turned against those on deck. This so enraged Anne Bonny that she ran to an open hatchway, cursed them all for cowardly dogs and then fired both her pistols into the hold, severely wounding several of her shipmates. All hands were either killed or quickly captured, and the two women were overpowered and put in leg irons. At the time of their capture, both Anne and Mary were wearing attack clothes—huge, baggy trousers and heavy, mannish blouses with scarfs tied about their heads. Their captors did not suspect their sex, and the women did not reveal it to them.

The British Chief Magistrate, having been sent over from England only recently, did not suspect their true sex either, and no one seems to have informed His Honor. Anne Bonny and Mary Read maintained their disguise throughout the entire trial in Port Royal.

When the trial reached its predictable conclusion and Calico Jack Rackham was sentenced to be hanged in chains, His Majesty's chief legal officer in the islands turned his bewigged head to the others standing huddled in the well of the court.

With a sarcastic edge to his voice, he asked if any of the others had anything to say concerning the question of whether they, also, should not be awarded a similar fate.

His Honor's eyebrows went up almost into his wig and his mouth dropped open in consternation as he beheld the youthful figures of two young pirates stride impertinently forward to address him.

"What possible reason could you two young scoundrels have to offer this Court as to why you should not be hanged by the neck until you are dead?" roared the Chief Magistrate.

Matching the judicial officer stare for stare and scowl for scowl, Anne Bonny tossed her head defiantly and replied, "Yer Majesty, we pleads our bellies!"

The shout of raucous laughter that went up from the pirates fairly made the rafters ring. Here was raw courage in the face of certain doom and a broad joke to end it all with. This the brigands could appreciate, and each identified himself at that moment with the defiant Anne. This was the rabbit spitting in the hound dog's face.

His Lordship turned white with anger. Pointing a trembling finger at the two lonely figures standing before him, he asked, "What is the meaning of this impertinence? Have you no fear of the hereafter?"

"Right is right, Yer Majesty," replied Anne. "Ye knows the English law as good or gooder than we does. Ye knows it's against the law to kill an unborn child and an English child at that. We both be pregnant, and ye cannot hang us."

Examination proved her to be right. Both Anne Bonny Rackham and Mary Read were in a family way and, under English law, could not be executed until after the birth of their children. But the other pirates had no such excuse and were not to escape.

A few days before Calico Jack's execution, Anne was allowed to visit him in his cell. Far from offering any condolences or consolation, Anne viewed her husband with contempt. "If ye had only fought like a man when the Britishers boarded us," she said, "ye might have died like a man instead of being hanged like a dog!" With that, she turned and flounced out of the cell. It was the last time she ever saw him.

Some time later, on the appointed day, Calico Jack Rackham, dressed in his bright and colorful calico trousers, was hanged in chains at high noon in the public square of Port Royal. His male crewmen were similarly dispatched a few minutes later, not only as a punishment for their crimes, but as a deterrent to others who might be tempted to go a-pirating.

Unlike Anne, Mary Read pleaded for her husband both at and after the trial. Swearing that the two of them had intended to forsake a life of piracy and settle down ashore, she begged clemency, but in vain. It did her no good to plead that she herself was responsible for forcing her husband into piracy and that he had no choice in the matter. He was hanged with the rest of them.

Mary contracted a fever soon after this and died in prison, attended to the end by Anne Bonny. Her child was never born. Mary's remains rest to this day in the beautiful little cemetery in Port Royal, where the soft trade winds blow over her grave and the tropic sun she loved so much shines down with a languorous warmth. She is remembered as "poor Mary Read" by the islanders. True to her colors to the end, she is said to have remarked shortly before her death that it was good that the penalty for piracy was death by the gallows. "Otherwise," she said, "every cowardly milksop from here to hell might be led to try to belong to the Brotherhood of the Sea, since there would be no real penalty."

Anne Bonny was never hanged so far as is known. Transferred to the gaol in New Berne in the Providence of Carolina, she was delivered of her child in safety. Through the influence of her father's friends, she received stay after stay of execution and was allowed to keep her baby in the gaol with her. Finally, she was pardoned altogether and left the New Berne gaol a free woman.

What happened to her after that is anyone's guess. Did she give away her red-headed baby boy and go back to sea to resume her piratical ways? Did she settle down in coastal Carolina and end her days as a midwife or a charwoman? Did she ever inherit any of her father's considerable wealth, or was it all used up in buying her pardon?

These and many more such questions will probably remain forever unanswered. Anne Bonny fades from sight with her release from prison and her pardon from the King. Perhaps she found peace and some degree of happiness in her old age. Perhaps, just perhaps, that beautiful, young, raven-haired girl you saw helping her father with his shrimp trawl in Core Sound has the blood of Anne Bonny in her veins. It is entirely possible.

The Indian Gallows

from *Outer Banks Mysteries & Seaside Stories*

The American live oak, one of the most beautiful evergreens, is entwined in the history and legend of the Carolina coastland. Sturdy and majestic, it is said to grow one hundred years, live one hundred years, and die one hundred years. Be that as it may, there are many ancient specimens still beautifying the landscape, and one of them, located in the deep woods of Colington Island, just west of the Wright Brothers Monument, is the locale of one of the most persistent and touching legends of this storied region.

This tree is called the "Indian Gallows Tree," and it was one of two live oaks growing within ten feet of each other. In time, a large limb from one of the trees grew out in the direction of the other tree, and the tip of that limb actually pierced and grew into the trunk of its neighbor, until the entire joinder developed into a huge letter *H* with the cross-bar, or cross-limb, being a good ten feet off the ground. This cross-limb put out shoots from the top, giving the whole thing the appearance of a garlanded archway, with the top of the arch being almost perfectly level and parallel with the surface of the ground beneath. Thus the trees grew long before our land was formed into a nation, and thus they continued until the early years of the present century, when one of the majestic trees died and was cut and carved into small souvenirs by the people who visited the place and were fascinated by the story connected with it.

According to our legend, in 1711 the family of Robert Austin was cast ashore in a shipwreck on the Outer Banks of what was to become North Carolina. Luckier than most, the Austins were able to salvage many of their worldly goods with the help of a friendly hunting party of Tuscarora Indians. Their lives and their property safe, the survivors began looking for a place to settle and begin the process of carving their homestead out of the lush wilderness.

Here again the Indians were a great deal of assistance, transporting the new settlers in their canoes and pointing out likely locations.

Foremost among these newfound friends was the handsome son of the chief of the tribe, a young brave called Prince Roanoke. One of the chief attractions of the English family, at least in the eyes of Roanoke, was the Austins' beautiful daughter Elnora, a typical English beauty with deep blue eyes, a peaches-and-cream complexion, and a wealth of long, silky blonde hair. Elnora liked the young Indian prince and valued him as a true friend in this wilderness, but that was as far as it went with her. She was betrothed to one Henry Redwine, who had promised to follow her to the New World and make her his wife just as soon as he had worked out his apprenticeship to a silversmith and was free to leave England.

Finally a suitable place for the Austins' home was found on

the north end of Roanoke Island, and here they began clearing a small patch of ground, setting out net stakes in the nearby sound, and generally making ready to work a living out of the land and sea.

The weather was mild and the Indians continued to be friendly, so things began to look bright and hopeful for the little family of settlers in that good year 1711. Prince Roanoke visited the area often, and he and the young and beautiful Elnora took long walks together, communicating as best they could and dreaming the dreams of youth everywhere.

Roanoke could not conceal his love for the English maid and told her of it on one lovely moonlit night as they strolled on the peaceful, wave-lapped shore of the island. She heard him out, and, misty-eyed with empathy and understanding, she told him that her heart belonged to her English lover and that she must remain true to her vow. She was bound by her heart as well as her vow to await his coming to the New World and the establishment of their home. Heartbroken and ashamed, Roanoke returned to his home up the mighty river. Hope is the last thing that dies in a man, however, and in the months that followed he returned occasionally to visit with his kin on the island and to talk and walk again with his beloved Elnora.

If things were hopeful and bright in the Austin household, they were anything but peaceful in the heart and mind and in the dreams of old King Cashie, monarch of all the Tuscarora tribes and the father of the young Prince Roanoke. King Cashie hated the intruding whites with all his heart, and he never ceased to dream of the day when they would be driven from his once happy and uncongested hunting and fishing grounds.

History now records that it was in the year 1712 that he secretly began to form his "Tuscarora Confederacy," a joining together of the various Tuscarora families with the Coree

Indians and the Machapunga Indians to the south and east in a common bond of mistrust of the new settlers and resentment of their presence.

Finally, in 1713 a plan for the massacre of all the whites began to take shape. There were many councils held deep in the woods, where the various chiefs discussed strategy and the chances for winning such a war of extermination.

Prince Roanoke knew about these meetings, of course. He even attended some of them. He was familiar with his father's hatred of the white men, but he never really believed anything drastic would result from all these meetings and rantings. He avoided such gatherings when he could find a good excuse.

So it befell that the young prince was as much surprised as anyone when he learned that the Tuscarora Confederacy had evolved into a Tuscarora council of war. A definite plan had been made, and dates had actually been set for a concerted attack on all white settlements and outlying farms in the region. An intricate time schedule had been adopted to coordinate the various attacks.

All was to be done by stealth, of course, and every effort was to be made to take the whites by surprise and thus make their annihilation easier. No one—man, woman, or child—was to be spared. The war was to be treated as a holy war, and all must die.

Immediately Roanoke's thoughts turned to his beloved Elnora and the certainty of her fate when the raiding band assigned to her island should arrive at her small cabin. King Cashie had planned that his son and heir-apparent should take a leading part in the execution of these massacres, but the young brave had quite different intentions.

Slipping quietly away at midnight from his father's village up the mighty Chowan River, the young prince crept silently to where he had hidden his small, fast canoe. He shoved it off from the shore, sprang in, and moved out onto the broad bosom of the river. Heading downstream as rapidly as his paddle could drive him, he hurried toward the island where his beloved slept, quite unmindful of her grave danger.

On and on glided the small boat, with Roanoke trying to conserve his strength and yet gain as much distance as possible before the growing light of dawn forced him to hide on shore. There he rested and slept until the falling darkness sent him once again on his errand of mercy.

Arriving at long last at the island where he had left his beloved, he was startled and dismayed to see tall flames leaping skyward from the direction of the Austin homestead. Hiding his canoe in the tall marsh grass at the north end of the island, the young prince crept stealthily through the woods until he came near the clearing he knew so well. The scene that he had feared to find lay before his eyes. The Austin home and all the outbuildings were aflame, and there in the farmyard, gun in hand, lay the lifeless body of Robert Austin, the shaft of an arrow protruding from between his shoulder blades.

A few feet away lay the body of Mrs. Austin, one arm extended toward her husband as if in a final effort to help him before the crushing, mangling blow of the tomahawk had ended her dream of the good life in this new world. Neither body had been scalped. The Indians had not yet learned this grisly trick from renegade white men.

Elnora was not to be seen anywhere, nor were any of the raiding party in evidence. Unwilling to venture into the clearing from the comparative safety of the forest, Roanoke lay perfectly motionless and silent until the fires burned themselves out and darkness once again enveloped the scene. Still there was no trace of Elnora or of the raiding Indians.

One last chance remained. A little to the south of the northernmost tip of the island there was a hidden cave right at the water's edge where storm tides had carved out a large hole under the overhanging bank. Roanoke and Elnora had walked there many times during their visits together and, as far as he knew, only the two of them were aware of the cave's existence.

With downcast heart and faint hope, the young brave threaded his way through the underbrush until he came to the hidden mouth of the cave. It was pitch black inside and completely silent, but he dared not make a light. With a sigh of despair, he was turning away from the hiding place when he heard a sob, a very human sob, from that dark hole. Rushing to the very end of the cave, he found his Elnora safe and sound but almost hysterical with grief and fear.

Clasping her tightly in his arms, he rocked slowly back and forth and made little comforting noises until she became calmer. Finally she was able to sob out the account of how she had been at the edge of the clearing when she saw the raiding party of painted Indians descend on her homestead, kill her mother and father, and set fire to the buildings. In their frenzy and war lust, the Indians had not even seen Elnora in the darkness, and she had run blindly, not even knowing the way she ran, until she found herself at the cave. There she had hidden in mortal terror until the young prince had arrived.

Now the young couple was faced with the even greater danger of trying to avoid the raiding Indian war parties who were ravaging the isolated white settlements of the Albemarle. Their only hope lay in reaching Edenton, far up the broad reaches of the Albemarle Sound and the Chowan River. They now knew that capture would mean their torture and death by the traditional Indian method, being burned alive while strapped to a sturdy post or stake. Daylight travel was out of the question.

Their sole chance lay in traveling at night and hiding by day.

This is exactly what they did. Their first night of travel was made more secure, if much more difficult, by the arising of a great storm. Strong winds and driving rain hid them from spying eyes but also nearly swamped the little canoe and made it much more difficult to handle. Fortunately they had a following wind that drove the small craft before it like a ship on the ocean, sometimes almost driving it under the waves, but at other times causing it to plane over the following sea. All that stormy night the young Roanoke paddled and steered his canoe toward the Chowan while Elnora tried desperately to bail the boat with her cupped hands. It was a wild night.

As the cold, gray first light of approaching dawn spread across the eastern sky behind them, they beached their boat on a sand spit that projected from the shore. They disembarked and dragged the canoe up into the shelter of a dense pine forest. Roanoke then went back and, with a branch broken from a pine tree, carefully walked backward as he wiped from the sand the keel mark of the little boat and the footprints of the travelers. When he returned to the hiding place in the trees, even the most careful searcher would have been unable to tell that anyone or anything had passed that way.

Completely spent, the two young fugitives lay down on the forest floor and, cushioned by a centuries-old carpet of pine needles, dropped quickly into the deep sleep of exhaustion. Food was not a problem. They would have been too bone-weary to eat, even if they had had food. During the morning the wind subsided into a gentle southerly breeze, and the rain continued to fall steadily, hissing through the needles of the pine trees and dropping softly to the ground.

At sunset Roanoke awoke, and while Elnora slept, he carefully scouted the area. He found nothing to increase his apprehension, but he did discover some berries and some edible pine tree buds, which he carefully gathered just as long as he could see in the fading light. Returning to the canoe, he found Elnora awake and anxious to continue their journey. After eating their meager meal, the two climbed back into the canoe and resumed their flight toward what they hoped would be safety.

It was an hour before daybreak when the headland of Edenton loomed before them. They reached the town wharf just as the townfolk and fishermen were beginning to come out of their houses to begin another day's work.

Excitement and indignation buzzed through the little town as the story of the massacre and the flight of the survivors spread like wildfire. Well did they know, these pioneers in this lush wilderness, that vengeful old King Cashie would not delay long in trying to apprehend any fugitives from his raids and to wipe out the settlement on the banks of the Chowan. Attack, they knew, was imminent.

Riding at anchor in the wide harbor of Edenton, there lay a fat merchant ship that had arrived only hours before with a cargo of, among other things, powder and shot and several dozen muskets. It may well have been the passage of that very ship up the waters of the sound which so frightened the raiding Indians that they did not try to pursue Roanoke and Elnora in their frail canoes, if indeed they had any knowledge of the couple's desperate flight.

Wonder of wonders, at least for Elnora, not only did the ship contain supplies and weapons, but it also held the person of her beloved Henry Redwine, free from his apprenticeship and come to claim his bride and his future in the New World. For Henry and Elnora, happiness was complete. Their sorrow at the death of her parents was softened by the joy of their reunion.

Not so, however, for Roanoke. He now saw his last chance of winning the beautiful English girl fade away to nothing. He was also faced with what he knew would be the anger and malice of his own father, King Cashie. He was, indeed, a man without a family, without a hope for the future.

In Edenton, history tells us, preparations for defense went forward rapidly. Log walls were erected just outside the town and redoubts of earth were thrown up to give shelter to the defenders. There were those in the community who looked askance at the presence of the young Prince Roanoke in their midst as all this was going on. But he worked so willingly along with the settlers in the preparation of the defenses, even scouting the nearby forests daily for signs of approaching Indians, that the people began to accept him as their true ally. One by one, the murmurings against him ceased.

When the attack finally did come, it was fierce but short-lived. The settlers were too well organized, and their musket fire from behind both log and earthen walls was too devastating for the Indians to bear. They fell back, carrying their dead and wounded with them. What finally broke the spirit of the attackers was a well-placed cannonball from one of the deck guns of the armed merchant ship. The ball landed right in the midst of a group of Indians, killing several and breaking the leg of King Cashie himself.

They fell back in disarray and never again seriously threatened Edenton, which continued to be too well armed and disciplined for the forces the Indians could muster thereafter. Although raids on isolated farms continued, the uprising of the Tuscarora Confederacy had just about run its course.

There now began for the young Prince Roanoke a most frustrating and sorrowful time. He could not safely return to his own people, and yet he felt very much an outcast in the town of Edenton. Forgetting how well he had served them in the recent armed conflict, many of the whites distrusted him just because he was an Indian.

Elnora and her new husband were consistently kind and thoughtful toward the young brave and did their best to relieve his loneliness, but to little avail. Their very kindness served to deepen the pain of seeing his beloved happily married to another man.

Finally Roanoke decided to take the fateful step that would either solve many of his problems or else end them once and for all. He would return, an eighteenth-century prodigal son, to his father's tribe. He labored under no illusions about the cruelty of Indian justice. He knew his father's temperament, but after all, he was the only son of the old chief, and he believed that, in his own savage way, the old man loved him.

Days and weeks went by as the young prince prepared himself for his journey of homecoming. He searched the woods with persistence until he found just the perfect specimen of turkeycock to yield the golden-bronze feathers for his girdle and a splendid white heron to furnish the head decoration to which he was entitled by tribal law in recognition of his accomplishments as a youth. Prime quality doeskin for his cape and tanned otter furs for his loincloth were available from local trappers and hunters. Finally his ceremonial costume was complete and perfect according to Indian tribal protocol.

Roanoke looked every inch the chief as he stood on the wooded edge of Oakum Street in Edenton and bade good-bye to his white friends. Tears filled the eyes of the young brave and the newlyweds as they shook hands with friendly palms cupped on each other's shoulders. Finally, with a tremendous heave of his young shoulders, Roanoke turned away from his friends, walked to where his frail canoe floated, and paddled off eastward over the broad bosom of Albemarle Sound.

It seems almost certain that the young prince was shadowed from the very start and for almost the entire journey down the sound. At any rate, when he finally reached his father's village, a committee of young braves was waiting for him. He was roughly seized, carried into the Indian village, and forthwith tied to a man-high stake set deeply into the sand.

There he remained, without food or drink, until nightfall, when the neighboring chiefs began to arrive to convene the court that would decide his fate. Throughout all that day and during the entire night-long trial that followed, Prince Roanoke uttered never a word. He did not seek to defend himself or to offer excuses or reasons as subchief after subchief made long, emotional speeches accusing him of traitorous conduct, of being responsible for the failure of their holy war, and of being entirely false and untrue to his father, his tribe, and the Tuscarora Confederacy. One after another, they all demanded that he be put to death for his sins against his people. Some of the orators even went so far as to spit in his face and strike him with their ceremonial gourds. King Cashie uttered not one word in defense of his son.

Finally the vote was taken, just as the day began to break over the forest. The decision of the chiefs was unanimous—death to the traitor. Because of the young brave's royal heritage, the chiefs decided to allow the old king to decide the manner of his son's execution.

Rising to his feet, with all the glory of the rising sun spreading its light behind him, the ancient and crippled king denounced Prince Roanoke and, with no show of sorrow whatsoever, disclaimed him as a son.

"He has loved the white man well," intoned the old chief, "and he has reaped the reward of the white man's fickleness.

Let him, therefore, not be granted the ancient Indian execution of fire at the stake but, rather, the shameful death on the gallows by which the white thieves kill their own criminals." His voice rising to almost an hysterical scream, the vengeful old Cashie spat out, "Let the traitor be hanged by the neck until he is dead, dead, dead!"

With savage shouts of approval, the Indian braves seized the young prince again. They tore away the deerskin thongs binding him to the ceremonial post and threw them into the sand. With eager haste, they dragged him through the forest by the hair of his head, through brambles and thorns and across little creeks until they reached the giant oaks with the peculiar cross-branch between their trunks.

Hastily fashioning a noose of rope, they placed it around Roanoke's neck and threw the other end over the cross-branch. They hoisted the bound Roanoke, kicking, into the air and hanged him by the neck until he was indeed "dead, dead, dead." Thus ends the legend of the Indian Gallows Tree.

As early as the year 1846, Colonel William H. Rhodes of Bertie County published a poem entitled "The Indian Gallows," which concludes with the Indian trial as old King Cashie exclaims:

No! not the stake . . .
He loves the pale-face; brothers, let him die
The white man's death! come, let us bend a tree
And swing the traitor, as the Red-men see
The pale-faced villain hang; give not the stake
To him who would the Red-man's freedom take
Who from our fathers and our God would roam,
And strives to rob us of our lands and home!

They seize him now, and drag him to the spot
Where death awaits, and pangs are all forgot.

There are those familiar with the area who say that the legend is not ended yet. They say that sometimes, when the moon is full and the wind is still, you will hear the sound of mourning and keening and weeping, and the little creek that runs by the gallows will run red as blood.

Blackbeard's Cup

from *Blackbeard's Cup and Stories of the Outer Banks*

"They say" that you should never tell a story in the first person. "They say" that it robs the story of some of its interest and that the teller limits himself unnecessarily. Well, "they" apparently have never heard of the popularity of true confession magazines and the appeal of the "I was there" approach. Anyway, there are some stories that cannot well be told in any other way.

The time was the very early nineteen-thirties, right in the middle of the late and unlamented "Great Depression." Nags Head and the remainder of the Outer Banks were still the "best kept secret" in North Carolina. There were miles and miles of undeveloped beaches on both the sound and the ocean sides of the famous barrier reef, and the whole area was as close to being a modern-day Garden of Eden as it could be. I was, at the time, a student in the law school at the University of North Carolina and already a veteran of nearly twenty summers of roaming and loving the Outer Banks.

Also in the same law school at the time was a young man

who shall be known here as only Jack to preserve his anonymity. He, also, was an habitué of this golden strand since childhood and was a member of one of the finest families in eastern North Carolina. At that time Jack was even more conversant with the legends of the region than I, particularly the regions around Ocracoke and Portsmouth Island. A lifelong friendship had grown between us, and we young blades spent countless happy and carefree days exploring these sands and drinking to the full the mystery and wonder of the area.

This was the picture on that happy August day when Jack came to me and said, "Charlie, I hope you've got ten dollars to spare because that will be your share of the cost of hiring a gas boat to take us to Ocracoke tomorrow as well as board and lodging for one night." I hadn't known we were going to Ocracoke at all, much less on the morrow but at that age in life, "theirs was not to reason why." After all, what was there to lose besides a lazy summer day? It put a tremendous dent in my pocketbook but I just happened to have that amount on hand so, without question, the deal was made and the trip planned. I had no idea what Jack had in mind, but a trip to Ocracoke was pleasant at any time and even then the price seemed a bargain.

Why not a car? In those days very few people could afford a car, and most of the ones who were affluent enough to try the trip over land and inlet usually got stuck in the sand. The ferries were adequate for the traffic at the time, but such an undertaking was fraught with danger and delay and frequent calls to the Coast Guard for an overland rescue. No, a boat was slower sometimes, but usually very pleasant and more dependable. Given the wind direction and force and the type and location of the clouds, you could estimate the time of your arrival at any given point on Albemarle or Pamlico Sounds with fairly reasonable accuracy.

The next day dawned clear and mild, and an early departure from the long pier jutting out from Hollowell's store and Post Office into the sound was made with high spirits and keen anticipation. There was no shade or awning on the Dutch Net boat we had hired and no relief from the blazing August sun, but all the voyagers were young and strong and already tanned a deep mahogany, so it made little difference. After all, who knew what adventure might lie ahead? We had practically no money to spare, but we were young and almost disgustingly healthy and it was summer and we were at Nags Head! The copious lunch we took along was consumed before the sun reached the zenith and the trip southward was without notable event. After we ate, we rescued some chicken bones from the drumsticks, threaded them onto hooks, attached a crab line we found in the boat, and trolled for bluefish. We caught a fairly nice mess of fish which we gave to our "skipper."

Ocracoke landfall was made well before dark, and the smooth water of Silver Lake beckoned us to a safe landing at the pier. The short walk to the Pamlico Inn was rewarded by the usual cordial welcome from the Gaskills and we settled in for supper.

After a bountiful seafood supper, we stepped out into the gathering dusk of a beautiful Ocracoke evening and breathed deeply of the soft, salty breeze which was coming in from the eastwards. Up to that point I had not known that there was any special purpose to our journey. Just a trip "down to Ocracoke" with all its nostalgic sights and sounds and smells was reason enough, not to mention the wonderful people who were part and parcel of it all. Pleasures were simple at that time and in that place but they were deep and soul satisfying. Even in those days it was like stepping back into history. That was part of the magic of Ocracoke.

“Come on,” said Jack, “we don’t want to be late.” When I demanded to know where we were going, he said, “To the castle.” “Are you crazy?” I asked. “Shell castle is out yonder in the middle of the sound and Jasper, our skipper, won’t be back until tomorrow morning!” “Take it easy, Chuck,” he replied. “There’s more than one castle around here, and the one we’re going to is Blackbeard’s castle. Come on with me.”

On we went down the picture-book streets of the town in the direction of Silver Lake. There were places where the branches of the trees met overhead, forming a sort of fragrant tunnel through which we walked. Jack apparently knew the way, and it seemed to me we walked a good while before we came to a large, white clapboard house with a sort of cupola or look-out tower on top, overlooking the waters of the sound. “This is it!” whispered Jack. “Look alive now and do exactly as I do and we may see something very few people ever get to see.”

Walking across the broad front porch, Jack knocked three times on the huge door with his clenched fist. The door swung slowly open, just enough for me to see a large, lantern-lit room and the silhouette of a tremendous, bearded man peering cautiously out of the cracked door. “What is it you want?” growled the giant. To my amazement, Jack immediately answered, “Death to Spotswood.” The eyes of the bear flashed to me. “And you?” he asked. Flabbergasted, I stammered the same thing Jack had said or as close to it as I could manage. That apparently, was some sort of password, because the heavy door swung open and we walked in. Only my unwillingness to leave Jack in such a spot prevented me from bolting for the door and back to the inn as fast as I could run.

The room we entered had obviously been used at one time as a dining room or banquet room. With high ceilings and beautiful wood paneling, its only furnishings now consisted of a very large oak table in the middle of the room surrounded by a number of rather modern-looking bentwood chairs. The only illumination came from a huge kerosene lantern placed in the middle of the table. Its soft, warm light revealed about a dozen of the biggest, toughest-looking men I have ever seen. Most of them were heavily bearded with flashing blue eyes, and every one of them spoke with that Elizabethan inflection so usual on this coast, which has been called "hoi toide talk."

As the first order of business, Jack and I were required to place our hands on a large Bible and to take a solemn oath that, under penalty of death, we would not reveal anything that went on in that room that night for thirty-five years. With a shiver of mixed anticipation and apprehension, I took the oath and settled back into one of the chairs near the table. Jack did likewise. The others in the room did not take the oath but they took similar seats and for a short while we heard nothing but the buzz of several different conversations.

All at once and as though on signal, an abrupt silence engulfed the room as a door at the far end swung slowly open and the bearded giant who had admitted us strode in, holding aloft a large, silver cup of a most peculiar shape. Handing it to the man at the head of the table, he sat down and the man holding the cup raised it ceilingward and in a deep resonant voice chanted, "Death to Spotswood!"—the same phrase that had gained us admission to the house. So saying, he took a long draught of the liquid in the cup and passed it to the man next to him, who did the same thing and said the same words. The cup then was passed from hand to hand around the table until it came to me. Thrusting the cup against chest, my neighbor fixed me with a stare so fierce and so demanding that my knees began to quiver. Too afraid to do anything else, I lifted the cup as I had seen them do and, in the lowest voice I could muster, repeated the words. Lowering the cup, I drank a large swallow of the amber liquid. My mouth and throat burned as if on fire! I gagged and coughed and finally managed to swallow, while the eyes of all that group were upon me. The stuff had not seemed to bother them at all.

While the silver cup was in my hands and before I passed it to Jack, I noticed it was of a very peculiar shape. Much larger than any drinking cup or chalice I had ever seen, it was nearly so large as a punch bowl and was relatively shallow for its width. At two places on its lip there were cup-shaped depressions in the edge about three inches apart, which sloped inward and made drinking from that side of the cup very difficult. I had quickly discovered that the potion we were drinking was some of the strongest corn whiskey I had ever sampled. It had a kick like a Missouri mule and that first swallow almost floored me.

Well, the evening wore on and the cup made round after round of the huge table. Frankly, I was scared not to take my part in the goings on, but I took as small sips of the potent liquor as I thought I could get by with. After a few rounds of the table, the talk loosened up and became more informal, and that night I heard some of the wildest tales about Edward Teach, the pirate, you can imagine. By that time we were on a first-name basis, but I never once heard the surnames of any of those present.

Fairly early in the evening I was enlightened to the fact that the oblate spheroid shape of the cup was due to the cup's being the silver-plated skull of Blackbeard himself. I became a little queasy when it dawned on me that, if the cup was a skull, then the little dips in its lip had to be the eye sockets! Carved in rather rough Elizabethan letters around the outside of the cup were the words "DETH TO SPOTSWOODE." Just how long the wild tales and the loving cup lasted I have no idea. Jack and

I made the excuse that we needed to go outside to get some fresh air. Once outside, we made the best speed we could to our lodgings and an exhausted sleep.

Jasper was back with his gas boat bright and early the next morning, and we made our way northward to Nags Head and a safe landing on the soundside. Little did we know that Blackbeard's castle and the Pamlico Inn and the Wahab house would be either destroyed or damaged beyond repair by the hurricane that struck Ocracoke in 1944, but such was to be the fate of these and several other well-known buildings on that historic island.

Afraid to discuss our adventure in front of Jasper, Jack and I waited until we were ashore before we started talking it out. We figured the oath did not forbid our discussing it with one another—only with nonparticipants. It turned out that Jack was almost as ignorant of what the strange affair meant and how it came to be as I was. A long-time "Banker" friend had given him the password and told him when and where to show up if he wanted to see something he probably would never see again. Acting on the trusted word of that friend, Jack had led us into the adventure.

We had both heard many times that Blackbeard's severed head had been coated with silver and made into a punch bowl and used by some Virginia families. We knew, of course, that the royal governor Spotswood, who had brought about Blackbeard's death, refused to return to England after his term of office expired because he feared (and probably rightly) that Blackbeard's friends, the Brethren of the Coast, would learn of it, intercept him at sea, and avenge the death of their friend and leader.

We kept our oath, Jack and I. At least, I feel sure that he did and I know that I did. It has now been more than fifty years and I figure I have done my part to keep their confidence. I can see no harm and no oath violation in disclosing this now. I don't even know whether any of the party who met that night is alive, but I do know the castle is no longer there.

In the trials and tribulations of pursuing a career in the law, the memory of the schoolboy adventure almost faded from my memory. One day recently I was looking through some old books I had inherited and I came across Crecy's *Grandfather's Tales of North Carolina History*, which was written back in the eighteen hundreds and was published by Edwards and Broughton. The author, Richard Benbury Crecy, lived closer to Blackbeard's time than we do, and he had devoted a section to the pirate. A perusal of the book proved Crecy to be a very accurate and a very complete portrayer of the history of this state. In his chapter on Teach he writes:

> Teach had seventeen desperate men under him. Maynard had more than thirty. The engagement was desperate. By a feint, Maynard's men were sent below and Teach was made to believe that Maynard declined the fight and was about to surrender. When Teach saw this, he sailed to Maynard's ship to take possession of her. As soon as he boarded, Maynard ordered his men on deck and then it was a hand to hand fight, Maynard and Teach heading it with sabers. Teach was mortally wounded after he had wounded twenty of Maynard's men. After Maynard had captured Teach's sloop, he cut off his head, fastened it to his bowsprit and sailed up to Bath in Beaufort County, then Hyde.

No mention here of carrying the head back to Virginia! And remember, Bath was Blackbeard's hometown. A great majority of the people there were his friends, including Governor Eden. In fact, Eden had performed Blackbeard's marriage ceremony just weeks before when he took a local bride. Maybe the severed head did not go to Virginia after all! Maybe it was "rescued" by some of the many friends of the pirate, and maybe it was them or some local silversmith who fashioned it into a silver cup bearing the curse on Spotswood. Perhaps the account of a punch bowl being made from the skull was a garbled one. What human has ever had a skull big enough to be used as a punch bowl? Maybe that odd-shaped, shallow bowl from which I drank was, indeed, the genuine article. Remember the secrecy with which it had been displayed and remember the location. Was it really the skull-bowl? I had to find out.

From that day to this I have tried as opportunity arose to trace the whereabouts and ownership of the bowl. Twice I thought I was on the verge of finding it, once in Norfolk and once in Virginia Beach, only to have the trail go cold. Both times it was rumored to be the property of a very rich Virginia collector, but when I tried as discreetly as I could to find him, I ran into a solid wall of silence.

I have discussed this search with my internist, a medical man in whom I have the utmost confidence, and he also has become interested. He tells me that if I can obtain possession of the object for only a few hours, he will help me have it X-rayed to determine if, indeed, there is a human skull underlying the silver plating. Before I meet my Maker I would greatly like to determine whether the silver bowl from which I drank is truly the skull of the famous pirate. The only way I know to do this is to obtain the cup so that it may be X-rayed, even if I am supervised and even if it is a brief loan.

In one final effort to do exactly that, I make this offer. I will pay one thousand dollars in cash to the person who loans me the cup from which I drank and I promise I will keep it just long enough to have it X-rayed. I will post a bond for its safe return and I pledge never to reveal the name and/or address of the owner. There is no chance of a counterfeit being run in on me. I held the cup in my hands and I drank from it and I shall immediately recognize it if I ever see it again. My friend Jack has long ago passed to his reward or I would certainly enlist his help in the search. Maybe, from where he is now, he already knows whether the cup is the genuine article, but I surely would like to know.

I surely would.